DEADLY INVITATION

"Just step back into the alley real easy-like, and keep your hands up where I can see 'em."

Ki did just as he was told. He would never risk doing anything that might endanger Jessie's life.

Jessie also backed up into the recesses of the alley. She kept her hands up high, but slowly turned around. She couldn't get a clear look at the man; the moon, still low in the sky, shed no light into the alley. But there was no mistaking the two silver gun barrels that were pointed right at them. "The Two Gun Kid!" she practically gasped.

"At your service," the Kid said engagingly. "The hunters become the hunted—poetic justice," he postulated freely. Even in the dark his eyes seemed to twinkle.

"What do you know about justice?" Jessie snapped.

"I spent enough years in prison to know all about it." There was little rancor in his words. "What do *you* know about justice?" he continued. "No more than you have to, and no more than it pays."

Also in the LONE STAR series
from Jove

LONGARM AND THE LONE
STAR LEGEND

LONE STAR ON THE
TREACHERY TRAIL

LONGARM AND THE LONE
STAR VENGEANCE

LONGARM AND THE LONE
STAR BOUNTY

LONE STAR AND THE
HANGROPE HERITAGE

LONE STAR AND THE
MONTANA TROUBLES

LONE STAR AND THE
MOUNTAIN MAN

LONE STAR AND THE
STOCKYARD SHOWDOWN

LONE STAR AND THE
RIVERBOAT GAMBLERS

LONE STAR AND THE
MESCALERO OUTLAWS

LONE STAR AND THE
AMARILLO RIFLES

LONE STAR AND THE SCHOOL
FOR OUTLAWS

LONE STAR ON THE TREASURE
RIVER

LONE STAR AND THE MOON
TRAIL FEUD

LONE STAR AND THE GOLDEN
MESA

LONGARM AND THE LONE
STAR RESCUE

LONE STAR AND THE RIO
GRANDE BANDITS

LONE STAR AND THE BUFFALO
HUNTERS

LONE STAR AND THE BIGGEST
GUN IN THE WEST

LONE STAR AND THE APACHE
WARRIOR

LONE STAR AND THE GOLD
MINE WAR

LONE STAR AND THE
CALIFORNIA OIL WAR

LONE STAR AND THE ALASKAN
GUNS

LONE STAR AND THE WHITE
RIVER CURSE

LONGARM AND THE LONE
STAR DELIVERANCE

LONE STAR AND THE
TOMBSTONE GAMBLE

LONE STAR AND THE
TIMBERLAND TERROR

LONE STAR IN THE CHEROKEE
STRIP

LONE STAR AND THE OREGON
RAIL SABOTAGE

LONE STAR AND THE MISSION
WAR

LONE STAR AND THE
GUNPOWDER CURE

LONGARM AND THE LONE
STAR SHOWDOWN

LONE STAR AND THE LAND
BARONS

LONE STAR AND THE GULF
PIRATES

LONE STAR AND THE INDIAN
REBELLION

LONE STAR AND THE NEVADA
MUSTANGS

LONE STAR AND THE CON
MAN'S RANSOM

LONE STAR AND THE
STAGECOACH WAR

LONGARM AND THE LONE
STAR MISSION

··◆ WESLEY ELLIS ◆··

LONE STAR

AND THE
TWO GUN KID

A JOVE BOOK

LONE STAR AND THE TWO GUN KID

A Jove Book/published by arrangement with
the author

PRINTING HISTORY
Jove edition/February 1987

ISBN: 0-515-08884-6

To Wiley, an outlaw to the end

Chapter 1

Only the soft crying marred the serenity of the afternoon.
The sun was shining brightly, but under the thick green
canopy of the stately old oak a gentle breeze cooled the air
pleasantly. All in all, it would have been a perfect day—
for anything but a funeral.

The minister's full-bodied voice had bestowed the
blessings on the deceased and was now busy elucidating
the man's good qualities. But Jessie Starbuck hardly listened. She stared at the pine-box coffin and was consumed
by her own thoughts. The impressively attractive woman
had come from her ranch in Texas to attend the funeral of
her friend, Eugene Dixon—once Marshal Dixon, now
simply the dear departed Mr. Dixon. Jessie brushed a lock
of her tawny blond hair back from her smooth forehead.
She had seen many a man buried in the dirt—many long
before their time. As a lawman, Marshal Dixon was well
aware of the dangers. He faced them every day, and he
faced them bravely. He knew death could find him at any
moment, and when he finally hung up his silver star he

thought himself lucky for having beat the odds for so many years. With his wife, his daughter, and a well-earned pension, Eugene Dixon retired to his modest spread to lead the quiet existence of a small rancher. Therefore, it was ironic that death—in the form of two bullets in his back—had finally caught up with him.

The scraping of the dirt falling on the wooden casket brought Jessie back from her private thoughts. Her cool green eyes studied the rather large assembly of mourners. The marshal was a respected, well-liked man. He made friends easily, and even more important, remained loyal and true to his friends. Yet someone had found a reason to want him dead.

Standing beside her was Ki, a tall, muscular gentleman garbed in a somber black suit. Underneath his matching black Stetson, only his almond-shaped eyes and slightly sallow complexion spoke of his Japanese lineage. His mother was Oriental nobility, his father, an American businessman. Despite the fact that his build was Caucasian, Ki's way of thinking was almost totally Oriental. Ki viewed death differently from his American companions. It was not the end of the line, but rather the continuation of a journey. His personal beliefs allowed him to look upon death stoically—even his own death. But those same beliefs also led him to fight strongly for justice.

". . . In the eyes of the Lord, no evil deed goes unpunished," the minister's voice rang out solemnly, his words spoken with complete faith and conviction. "For in the end, we must all stand before our Maker . . ."

Ki did not necessarily disagree with the minister's words, but thought more in terms of fate and destiny than in terms of an Almighty. And though he agreed that in the end all wrongs were righted, he could not separate himself from the role he often played assisting fate to set the record straight. After all, he had his destiny to live out as well, and if fate had him serving as an agent of justice in the here and now, that was fine with him. He began to wonder what

2

fate now had in store for him and Jessie. One thing was certain, Jessie Starbuck would not let the murder of a friend pass easily.

Just then Ki spotted the reflection of the sun in the distant hills. It could be reflecting innocently off a piece of mica or some other mineral substance embedded in a rock, or it could be the reflection off a gun barrel or a pair of field glasses. There was no telling for sure, but Ki was alert to the possibilities.

The service ended and the mourners passed by the grave and paid their respects to the grieving widow and daughter. Jessie hung back till most of the gathering had left before she went up to the Widow Dixon. She was always unsure what to say at such occasions; mere words never seemed to express her feelings adequately, but she knew that was no reason not to try. She approached the woman. "Mrs. Dixon, I truly wish there was..."

She was cut short as the widow drew Jessie to her. "Jessie, Jessie, I'm so glad you could make it," she said in between sobs. "Eugene would have been so pleased."

"I wouldn't have missed it, Mrs. Dixon, you know that."

"Now, Jessie, I won't have you standing on formalities, especially at a time like this. It was always Nell to you," she said with a smile.

Jessie nodded and smiled at the woman. For all her years worrying about her husband, Nell had aged well. With her gray hair tied back in a tight bun, she had the attractive demeanor of a sophisticated older woman, though her sweet voice and warm smile still held all the charm of her younger years. Nell turned to introduce the young lady who stood next to her. "Jessie, I don't believe you ever met our little girl, Katie."

"She's hardly a little girl," Jessie said with a smile. Katie was tall and slender, with long flowing curls of light-brown hair that added to her majestic stature. She had the blue eyes of her father and the high cheekbones of her

3

mother. There was no denying it, Katie Dixon was a very pretty young lady. "Your father has told me so much about you. It's a pleasure to finally meet you." Jessie regretted her choice of words almost immediately. At the mere mention of her father, Katie's lower lip began to tremble and tears welled up in her eyes. "I'm sorry," Jessie added quickly. "I wish it were under different circumstances."

"We all do, Jessie," Katie replied with a feeble smile. "Daddy spoke often of you too, Jessie. I'm surprised we never met before."

"The last few times I came through you were back East."

Katie nodded. "Living with my aunt in Boston." As she spoke her eyes wandered to the gentleman who stood next to Jessie.

"This is Ki," Jessie said simply.

Hat in hand, Ki stepped forward and took hold of Nell's outstretched hand. "I met your husband in El Paso; he was a good man, Mrs. Dixon."

"He felt the same about you, Ki. But it's Nell to you as well."

"All right, Nell." Ki turned to Katie, "My deepest sympathies, ma'am."

"It's Katie to any friend of my father's," Katie said sweetly.

"You are your father's daughter," Ki observed aloud. "You have the same deep-blue eyes."

"Why, thank you, Ki." Katie curtsied politely. As she straightened up, Jessie could detect the faint trace of a modest blush. Dryly Jessie wondered if Katie had learned that at finishing school back East.

"You'll be staying at the house with us?" Nell asked, though it was more an invitation than a question.

"We've already checked into the hotel," Jessie said apologetically.

"That's foolishness," Nell continued.

4

"We didn't want to be a burden to you, Nell. We knew you would be busy."

"Then come back to the house with us now. Please, Jessie. There are some things I'd like to ask of you."

"Of course, Nell. Anything you need, don't hesitate . . ."

"Not here. We'll talk at home." Nell's sweet voice was all seriousness.

"I'll help you to your wagon," Jessie said as she took hold of Nell's arm. Katie came around on her mother's other side and, arm in arm, the three women left the cemetery. Ki followed quietly behind.

The Dixon house was an unassuming log construction of a type popular throughout the region. Simple on the outside, it was nevertheless comfortably furnished. Though far from being lavish, the little touches—lace curtains, linen doilies, and braided rugs—added to the interior's warmth and charm. Nell had done a nice job with her home.

They sat in the main room of the house, Jessie and Ki on the large floral-print sofa, Nell in a sturdy, straight-backed rocker. Across from the fireplace was a thickly padded leather chair, no doubt Eugene's seat of choice. Nell waited for Katie to finish serving the tea before addressing her. "Katie, why don't you show our guest around the place. There's not much to see, Ki, but it's all ours."

"Nell, anything you want to say you can say—" Jessie began, but then stopped abruptly. She had naturally assumed that Nell was hesitant to discuss certain matters in front of Ki. Jessie was about to inform Nell that Ki was totally and completely trustworthy, when she realized that it was not Ki she wanted to leave the room but her daughter Katie.

Ki rose to his feet, but seemed unconvinced as to what he should do. "We'll be okay," Jessie assured him.

"Oh, go ahead, Ki," Nell added. "It'll sure beat sitting

around drinking tea with the womenfolk."

Ki refrained from remarking that he didn't consider drinking tea a womanly habit, or a waste of time, but with a polite bow excused himself and followed Katie out the door.

Nell put down her cup and turned to Jessie. "This is not an easy thing to ask . . . I didn't want to discuss it in front of Katie. I was afraid it would only disturb her further."

"I understand, Nell. And I think I know what you're getting at."

The older woman looked surprised. "You do?"

Jessie nodded. "The Circle Star is at your disposal. When we get back to town I'm going to cable my foreman and have him send up some ranch hands. I don't want you to worry in the least about the roundup."

Nell smiled, but did not seem any too relieved. "Jessie, that's awfully kind of you—"

"I mean it, Nell. You have enough on your mind as it is."

"But I can take care of the ranch just fine," continued the widow. "Don't look so surprised. You're not meanin' to tell me ranching is not woman's work, now are you?" she added with a grin.

"Now, how could I tell you that, Nell? If you ask me, I think we women were cut out for ranching. I was just looking a bit surprised because, with the marshal gone, I was certain you'd be needing help around here."

Nell nodded. "Oh, without Eugene it'll be harder, all right. He did most of the work himself, but hired seasonal hands when he needed them. I reckon I'll manage the same."

"I know you can, Nell," Jessie added encouragingly.

"But I need another kind of favor from you. Something I can't manage myself."

"Go ahead," urged Jessie.

Despite Jessie's invitation, Nell was still having difficulty. She fidgeted with her teacup and did not look at

Jessie as she talked. "I don't know what you know of Eugene's death . . ."

"I've heard talk around the hotel."

"Then you know he was murdered!" Nell's voice was stronger, her words came out easier. Jessie nodded. "I want the man brought to justice." Again Jessie nodded, but said nothing. Nell fell silent, and when she spoke again her voice was quiet and unsure. "You don't think that's wrong of me?"

"Of course not, Nell."

"But it won't bring Eugene back," Nell said painfully.

"No, it won't."

"Then what's the point? Revenge?"

"No, justice," Jessie replied simply. "The marshal spent the greater part of his life fighting for that, Nell. He would want any killer, not only his own murderer, brought to justice."

"I know that, Jessie. That's why I want to enlist your help."

"I'll do everything I can to find out who killed your husband," Jessie promised.

"It won't be that hard, Jessie. I know who killed Eugene."

Katie and Ki stood on the ridge that rose behind the house. "Mama wasn't being modest when she said there was not much to see."

"There are the wildflowers," Ki pointed out. The field was carpeted with colorful daisies and sweet williams.

Katie smiled. "Daddy always used to say if people bought flowers, we'd be rich . . ." Her voice trailed off, and she fought to keep back the tears. Once she regained her composure, she continued, "Our land ends at that row of hickory trees, at least officially it does. Most of our neighbors also own small spreads, and by common consent, they've kept the range open and free."

"That suit everyone?" Ki asked aloud.

"I imagine so, or they'd do something about it."

Ki wondered if someone wasn't already doing just that.

"The thing about an open range is that it benefits everyone equally," Katie continued. "So it seems to me that most people would be satisfied with it."

Most, except for that one greedy individual, Ki thought to himself.

"Well, now that you've seen this, I guess I'll show you the barn." She started down the hill, then turned and let out a soft chuckle. "I don't think it was mama's intention for me to give you the tour. She just didn't want me to hear her discussion with Jessie. She still treats me like a little girl." She paused and seemed to want some response from Ki. When none was forthcoming, she continued coyly, "You don't think I'm a little girl, do you, Ki?"

"I think there's always a bit of a little girl in every woman," he said cryptically.

Katie thought that over for a moment, then seeming satisfied continued briskly to the barn.

As they entered the barn, Katie turned to Ki with a smile. "When I *was* a little girl I used to help my father pitch hay." Her foot kicked at the mound of hay as she reminisced out loud. "As a reward he would let me go up there, and then I would jump down into his arms. Of course he would never catch me; I'd fall right into the pile, clear up to my ears." This time as she stopped talking she broke out into tears. Ki didn't know if he acted first and put his arms around her, or if she first buried her face into his chest. Either way he was now cradling the crying woman close to his body.

Katie tried to talk, but could not get the words out between sobs. "Shh, don't say anything. It's all right," Ki said softly as he held her tight. She continued to cry. "Sit down, you'll feel better," he said as he tried to lower her to the hay. But she did not let go of him and they tumbled into the soft straw together.

Katie nestled up against him, and slowly her tears subsided. Ki could feel her warm breath against his neck, and the smell of her freshly powdered body. It was beginning to have its effects; he felt his pants beginning to shrink. With every breath she took, her small rounded breasts pressed against him. Even through the cloth of her dress and his jacket he could feel her nipples growing taut. That proved too much for him, and his organ swelled to life. Foolishly he hoped she would not notice his growing erection, but a bulge that size was impossible to ignore. He only hoped she would not take offense.

When her leg brushed against his erection, Katie gave a little shudder. For a moment Ki felt mortified and started to give a feeble apology, when Katie rolled on top of him, her pelvis pressing into him. Ki let out a soft groan. Immediately Katie raised herself off him. "I hope I didn't hurt you." Ki shook his head. "I'd like to just lie against you for a few moments, Ki. If you don't mind?"

Ki responded by stroking her soft hair. Katie lay back down on Ki, her thighs strategically placed on either side of his rigid shaft. It became quite clear she had no intention of just lying against him. Her hips began to rotate slowly, then picked up speed as she ground against him with more force. Her face was buried against his neck and Ki could feel her breath coming in forced gasps. Her movements had changed too. She wrapped her arms underneath his shoulders and with an arched back pulled herself up and down the length of his shaft. From her frantic, desperate writhings Ki realized it would not be long before she reached her climax. He ran his hands down her back and over her soft, rounded cheeks. The light pressure of his hands intensified her rasping breath. He squeezed her rocking bottom in his hands. She bucked twice, a tremor shaking her whole body. She let out a soft cry and lay still against him.

Ki was thinking she had fallen asleep when Katie lifted her head from his chest. "Thank you for holding me, Ki. I think I needed somebody to squeeze the tears out of me."

Ki was thinking that it wasn't the tears that were squeezed out of her. But he didn't say so.

"Ki, was it wrong for me to do that?"

"No, Katie, it wasn't wrong."

"But to feel such passion, especially today, right after the funeral . . ."

"You needed to be comforted, Katie."

"Don't you ever need to be comforted, Ki?" Her hand reached down to his still-hard shaft. "Does Jessie, I mean, do you—is it wrong for me to do this?"

"Katie, Jessie is like a sister to me. She and her father were, are, my only family, my only friends here."

Katie stroked his member. "I'm sure you're just being modest, Ki. You must have lots of women friends." She didn't let him answer but continued, "Oh, I don't mind, Ki. I just want to be your friend too."

Ki nodded. It was what Katie was waiting for. She hopped off him and quickly tugged at his pants, freeing his throbbing erection. Katie gasped. "It's so big, and red. I hope I didn't rub you raw." She lowered her head to his shaft and gently kissed its swollen tip. "Sometimes I think I should learn to be more gentle." Her fingers lightly caressed the length of his hard pole. "My aunt keeps telling me I'm not a tomboy anymore, and ladies should learn to be gentle." She lowered her mouth around his organ, her tongue dancing around playfully. "But then sometimes I still like to play rough." Her hand increased its pressure and she began to administer long, hard strokes to Ki's massive shaft. Her mouth resumed its position between Ki's legs, but this time she was anything but gentle as she sucked him in hungrily. "That's my problem, Ki. When you're born on the frontier, but get educated back East, you're never quite sure what to do." She flicked her tongue lightly against his tender, soft skin, her nails almost imperceptibly tracing patterns along his twitching organ.

"I think you know exactly what to do, Katie. I'm just

wondering if they taught you this at finishing school," Ki added playfully.

"It's amazing what they don't teach you. But I learned a little something about finishing. . . ." She took the base of his shaft in both hands and smiled at him warmly. Teasingly she brushed her cheek against him, then slowly slid him into her mouth—all the way into her mouth and down her throat.

Ki moaned, and involuntarily rocked his hips in time to her bobbing head. He could feel the exquisite pressure building up in his loins. Katie must have felt it too. She lifted her head briefly. "Yes, Ki, now!" she urged, then slid him back into her mouth. Ki needed no further encouragement. As his throbbing organ pressed against the back of her throat, he exploded.

Katie swallowed quickly as she tried to keep her mouth from being flooded. She sat up and wiped her mouth with the back of her hand. She smiled down at Ki warmly, but her smile turned to amazement as she noticed his shaft was still rock-hard and standing straight up in the air. "Why, Ki, maybe there's more to finishing than I thought," she said devilishly.

She rose to her knees and hiked her skirt up to her waist. "I think I'd like to lie down on you again. I promise it'll feel even better than before. I want you deep inside of me," she said as she lowered her moist tunnel onto his hard bone. She wasn't lying; it felt infinitely, indescribably better.

Chapter 2

"Considering there wasn't much to see, you were gone a long time," Jessie said to Ki as she climbed into the wagon.

Ki guided the team down the road that led from the Dixon place. A slow smile crossed his face. "That was mostly Katie's doing."

"I can imagine," Jessie said dryly, though without any trace of jealousy.

"She wanted to give her mother enough time alone with you."

"How considerate."

"I thought so. We managed to while away the time."

"Pleasantly, I hope."

"It was a rather pleasant afternoon," Ki agreed. "Katie can be quite charming," he added with a teasing smile.

"I hadn't noticed. Though I guess that's what fancy Eastern schools are for."

"I'm not so sure she learned it all in school. Some people are naturals," Ki said slyly.

12

Jessie turned on him sharply. "Ki, I'm not amused listening to—" She stopped abruptly when she saw Ki chuckling softly. "I don't know why I let you ruffle my feathers like that. You take pleasure in it, don't you," she accused openly.

"I meant what I said, Jessie. Take yourself for instance. You have more sophistication and allure than they could ever teach in a school. Some people are way beyond studying the art of eloquence and charm—"

"And some are so adept at it they should be teaching it, or should I say shoveling it." She knew there was no reason to be testy with Ki, and it surprised her the way she snapped at him. Ki had never been jealous over the many men she had met and loved. She studied her handsome companion closely; at least he never appeared jealous. "Ki, I'm sorry I snarled at you. I had a disturbing conversation with Nell."

"I thought as much. I figured a little playful teasing might pull you out of your mood."

Jessie turned away and stared up at the cloudless sky. The sun was low to the horizon, already below the nearby hills, and the sky was aglow in warm shades of red and orange. It promised to be a beautiful sunset, but Jessie was unmoved. Seeing a good friend into the dirt was never a pleasant experience. At the hotel, she would take a cool bath, and let the water refresh her weary body and mind. She turned back to Ki. There was not a crease or wrinkle in his smooth forehead, yet his eyes remained ever vigilant. Jessie drew strength from her companion; her weariness faded and was replaced with a knowing contentment. Ki had always been there when she needed him. She hoped he always would be.

"Well, let's just say I'm glad you had a pleasant afternoon," Jessie said sincerely.

"I wasn't totally idle."

"I wouldn't think so, Ki," she said with a teasing grin.

"I think I may have turned up some information about

13

Marshal Dixon's shooting."

"Oh?" Jessie asked curiously.

Ki nodded and began to tell her about the open grazing land, and his suspicions that one of the neighbors, in an effort to gain more land for himself, might have resorted to murder. "I keep thinking of the funeral gathering, and wondering which one of those people would have wanted to see the marshal dead," he said in conclusion.

"That's interesting speculation, Ki. But unless any of the mourners went by the name of the Two Gun Kid you'd be barking up the wrong tree."

"The Two Gun Kid?" Ki said questioningly. "I never heard of him."

"That doesn't mean he didn't shoot the marshal."

"No, of course not," agreed Ki. "But what makes you think it's him?"

"A few years back, Marshal Dixon arrested the Two Gun Kid. Two weeks ago, he was released from Leavenworth. He came directly here."

"Sounds guilty," Ki pronounced flatly. His words surprised even himself.

"I don't know if you're being sarcastic or not, Ki." Ki wondered about that himself, but did not comment. Jessie continued. "We have a man with a good motive, in the right place at the right time."

"It's certainly worth looking into. Do they have a posse out after the man?"

"There's no need. The Two Gun Kid is still in town."

"I suppose he had an ironclad alibi?"

"No one knows; he wasn't even questioned," Jessie informed him.

"That's odd."

"Isn't it? The sheriff says he won't arrest Two Gun without proper evidence."

"Are there other suspects? Maybe the sheriff is working on something we don't know about?"

"There's not a one, Ki. But that's not all. Before the

14

marshal was killed, men in the bar heard two shots come from the alley. Two shots that sounded almost like one."

Ki nodded his head slowly. "The Two Gun Kid's trademark?"

"Right," Jessie confirmed. "He earned his name, and his reputation, for being equally fast on the draw with either hand. It's said he can accurately empty two guns before most men can clean out one."

"Is it true?" Ki asked.

"I don't know."

"It doesn't really matter, as long as he has the reputation for it. It's starting to make some sense now. The sheriff is scared of the outlaw."

"Law or no law, it wouldn't be the first time a gunman bullied his way around a town."

"Then until someone comes up with some solid evidence, the Two Gun Kid goes scot-free."

Jessie looked squarely at Ki. "What can we do?"

"We can find the proof, and bring the killer to justice," Ki announced resolutely.

Jessie smiled. "That's just what I told Nell."

Just then there was a rifle crack up ahead. Ki snapped the reins and the team raced ahead. There was another shot, and a riderless horse galloped past. In the dirt ahead lay the sprawled figure of a man.

Jessie hopped down from the wagon before it had come to a stop. She had just reached the body when the dust exploded at her feet. The next thing she knew, Ki's arms were around her and they went rolling through the dirt. They came to a stop ten yards from the fallen man's body.

"Keep your head down," Ki ordered. Jessie had little choice; Ki's muscular arms were gently but effectively keeping her nose pressed into the soft ground. "When I count to three we're going to make a dive for that log." Ki allowed Jessie to turn her head enough to see the fallen oak that lay just a few feet from them. "Ready . . ."

They made it to safety without another shot being fired.

15

"Do you think he's gone?" Jessie asked.

"I don't know," Ki answered. "There's one way to find out," he said as he raised up on his heels.

Jessie placed a restraining hand on his arm. "There's a better way than exposing you to his fire." She pulled up her skirt and removed an ivory-handled derringer that was strapped to her shapely thigh. "My Colt would be better, but I think this should work."

"Jessie, there isn't a woman this side of Annie Oakley who can shoot like you, but it has to be a good hundred yards to those trees. If he's hiding in there, you might just as well spit at him as try to hit him with that."

"Why, Ki, I think your 'pleasant afternoon' has affected your reason. Now just hush up and watch." Jessie quickly lifted her head above the log and fired off the two quick shots of her tiny gun. The sound was a feeble pop compared to the solid boom of a good six-shooter, but it served its purpose. Jessie's shots were quickly answered by the loud crack of a rifle. With her head back down behind the tree trunk she smiled triumphantly at Ki.

"Very good, Jessie. Like I was saying," he added with a smile, "there isn't a woman I know of with your cunning."

"Of course it's good," she admitted boldly. "I learned it from you."

Ki let out a laugh. "I don't know what's gotten into me." Jessie gave him an all-knowing look. Ki looked slightly embarrassed. "Well, maybe I do know, but it's not what you think," he said defensively.

"No?" Jessie said with raised eyebrows.

Ki looked away, presumably checking out their surroundings. "Sometimes when people start shooting at you, Jessie, I seem to lose my, ah, composure." It was now Jessie's turn to blush.

"Thank you, Ki, but there's still someone shooting at me, and I think it would be best if you maintain a clear head."

16

"I don't really think we're in too much danger," Ki said casually.

"Crouching behind a fallen tree, nose to the dirt, is not my idea of a pleasant evening. Especially when my hair is liable to be parted by a passing slug."

Ki smiled. "There's not much chance of that."

"Anyone who could down a rider could pick us off just as easily," Jessie protested.

"That's what had me puzzled as well. Mind you, I'm not looking a gift horse in the mouth, but I think we're more than lucky to have made it to shelter."

"What do you mean?" Jessie asked.

"I think our friend out there was a good enough shot to have hit one of us as we rolled behind this log. I just think that wasn't his intention."

"He sure had me fooled," Jessie said sarcastically. But then she thought it over and agreed with Ki. "Maybe you're right, but then why bother shooting at us at all?"

"There could be a couple of reasons. Maybe he doesn't want us to reach that man."

"That doesn't make any sense. He's stone-cold dead."

"Maybe our friend out there doesn't know that," Ki replied.

"Then why doesn't he put another couple of shells into him?"

"I don't think he can. Don't get up to look," Ki said matter-of-factly, "but the road dips slightly right where the body lies. It's possible that it's just out of the line of fire."

"Then we're pinned here until that bushwhacker knows his man is dead."

Ki nodded. "But it's only a matter of time. Without proper medical attention the man will eventually bleed to death."

Jessie rolled onto her back. "And how long do you suppose that would take?"

Ki thought aloud, "Lying unconscious with two bullets

17

in him, anywhere from two to eight hours, or until dark, whichever comes first."

"Now what does sundown have to do with bleeding?"

"Nothing," Ki informed her flatly. "But there's also the other possibility that our friend out there is just waiting for darkness to cover his exit."

"He's playing it awfully safe if he's afraid we might stick our heads up and spot him just as he takes off."

"The way I see it, he can play it any way he wants." Ki pulled down his jacket and stretched out his legs. "How long do you think till nighttime?"

Jessie looked up at the graying sky. "Not much more than an hour."

"See you then," Ki said as he closed his eyes. "It's been a tiring day."

"That's it? That's all you have to say?"

Ki opened his eyes and smiled. "I'm sorry your dress got ripped," he said apologetically, then, impervious to their situation, reclosed his eyes and drifted off to a peaceful rest.

A short time later he opened his eyes. "Of course, there is one problem—by now our team is probably back at the livery, feed bag already in place." Before Jessie could respond, he turned over and slid back into his calm repose.

As predicted, once they felt it safe to come out from the protection of the fallen oak, their friend with the rifle and their wagon and team were nowhere to be seen. It was dark, but both Jessie and Ki scoured the area they felt had concealed the gunman in hopes of finding a clue. Neither of them were surprised when they came up empty-handed.

Then came the walk back to the Dixon place, where after a brief stop for a meal of cold ham and beans, Jessie and Ki borrowed two horses and started back again to town. Nell had wanted them to spend the night, but Jessie was eager to get the dead man back to town to see if anyone could identify him. She had a sneaking suspicion his death might have something to do with the Two Gun Kid.

Put that way, Nell sent them on their way; she didn't want to hamper any efforts that might bring the outlaw to justice. Katie, though, had nothing to say on the matter. She had gone to bed early, and was asleep throughout their visit.

When Jessie and Ki arrived back in Coleville, the town, with the exception of the Silver Lode Saloon, was sound asleep. Ki accompanied Jessie to the hotel, then set off to try to learn the identity of the murdered stranger. On their return they had found the dead man's horse grazing near its slain owner, and they had loaded the corpse onto the extra horse. Ki now walked the horse over to the saloon and tied the animal to the hitching post. He slung the body over his shoulder and pushed through the batwings into the brightly lit saloon.

The Silver Lode was one of those saloons that tried to accommodate all tastes and pleasures and offered its patrons every kind of vice. There was liquor, simple food, music, and a small stage that come Saturday night was no doubt full of dancing girls. Upstairs, off the balcony, there were also a few rooms, though they weren't intended for putting up overnight guests. Rooms were probably booked by the hour, or as needed. But the biggest draw at this hour was the gambling tables set up in the front corner of the large main room.

Ki entered the saloon unnoticed, but by the time he set the body down on a table opposite the bar all eyes were on him. The room quieted down as men pointed and murmured to each other. Ki walked up to the bartender. "Recognize this man?" he asked casually.

The bartender nodded. "Hank Greene, works over in the stable. Least he used to. Where'd you find him?"

"On the road into town," Ki answered, but his attention was focused on the mirror that hung behind the bar. In it he studied the reactions of the other men. He hoped to spot someone who seemed either uninterested or overly surprised. That kind of reaction would not necessarily pinpoint the killer, but it might single out an individual who had prior knowledge of the bushwhacking. A man could be innocent, yet still know of someone who had a score to settle or a wrong to right. There might be someone in the room at this very moment who had wanted to see this man dead. For all he knew there might be a few men who had felt that way. Ki would never approve of the method, but he would reserve judgment till he knew more about the murder. Although he generally tended to side with the victim, it was quite possible that Hank Greene got what he deserved.

The bartender set a drink down in front of Ki. Ki didn't feel the necessity for the alcohol, but he accepted the gesture of good will, and downed the contents of the shotglass in one swallow. In return for the drink, the bartender expected the details of the story. Ki did not disappoint him. "He must have been bushwhacked right before sundown. I heard the shots, but when I got to him he was already dead." Judiciously, Ki chose to delete any mention of Jessie.

A crowd now gathered around Ki. Some came to gawk at the body of the stable hand, others came to listen to Ki's tale. Probably most moved closer for some of both.

"He's been shot in the back and again in the head," someone remarked coldly.

"No one deserves to die like that," added another.

Ki turned to the speaker. "Any idea who might want to see him dead?" There were a few grumbled responses, but no clear answer.

"He wasn't the most liked man in town. Mr. . . . ?"

"Ki. Why's that?"

"Hank had a mean streak in him, to horses and men alike. Most times he was all right, but when he got his dander up, or drank a bit too much, it was best not to cross his path. Still, that ain't a reason to gun a man down like that." Others in the crowd agreed.

"Someone had a reason," Ki said softly but clearly.

A short, leathery man pushed his way forward and stood defiantly before Ki. He had a narrow face covered with coarse stubble, and deep-set dark eyes. "That's your side of the story, mister." Ki studied the man. He wore his gun low, and had the look of a man who wouldn't hesitate to use it, but unlike a true gunfighter his hands were calloused enough to prove he also earned his keep doing some hard, and presumably honest, work. Ki did not respond, and the man continued. "You say you found him at sundown, so how is it you're just gettin' in now?" It was a good question, and others nodded their heads waiting for the answer.

"When I got down to help him, someone fired a shot at me and spooked my team," Ki explained calmly.

"A roan and a bay?" someone asked from the crowd. Ki nodded. "That explains the rig I saw coming in this evening."

"His story's straight, Tucker," confirmed another.

Tucker looked around angrily. He seemed undecided as to what to say next. In the mirror, Ki noticed a well-dressed man sitting at the card table give an almost imperceptible nod. As if given the cue Tucker tried another approach. "How do we know he ain't the one who shot Hank?" he said accusingly.

"Why would he do that?" asked a voice in the crowd.

"For his money," Tucker answered quickly. "Anyone notice, this fella ain't white, yet he's dressed better'n most of us?"

Ki had never known racial prejudice not to have an effect. Before, most of the crowd had seemed intrigued but indifferent, and had been unwilling to choose sides. But now their suspicions and fears came into play, and Ki could feel the atmosphere in the room slowly change. It did not bother Ki; perhaps in anger someone would let slip a remark or comment that would prove useful.

"I say we search him," someone shouted from the rear of the group. Other voices agreed. It was turning ugly fast.

21

"Hold your horses," the bartender's voice echoed with authority. "Hank never had an extra coin on him. You all know that. He's even into me for a couple weeks' worth of wages."

Apparently the bartender must have been right, for the tension in the air relaxed dramatically. But Tucker was not letting up. "I still say we should search him."

"What would be the point?" Ki said calmly. "Whatever you think I might have stolen from this man I would have surely hidden by now."

Ki's composure only served to irritate Tucker more. But when others started to agree, the small man's temper flared up. "I say this Chinee smells damned suspicious."

"Aw, give it up, Tucker," a man said as he walked back to the card table.

"Yeah, why would he shoot Hank, then bring him back here?" added another.

"Just so we wouldn't suspect him. There ain't no better way to throw the dogs off the scent than backtrack your own trail."

Ki had to admit there was a certain twisted logic to Tucker's reasoning. But he wasn't as interested in defending himself as he was in finding out why Tucker was so keen on pinning the murder on him. And where did the well-dressed gambler fit into all this? At the thought of the gambler, Ki glanced into the mirror and noticed that the card player was gone. Ki turned back to Tucker and decided to take a gamble himself. He stared straight into the man's eyes and spoke in a loud, clear voice. "And when the hounds are barking up the wrong tree, the fox can slip away."

"I don't like your tone, Chinee." Tucker turned to face Ki and broadened his stance. "Just what're you tryin' to say? Maybe I misunderstood your English."

"It's rather clear," Ki informed him gently. "I think maybe the real killer would be all too eager to blame it on a passing stranger."

22

The crowd quickly backed away from the two men. Ki prepared for the inevitable. He shifted his weight to his rear leg, ready to lash out with a front snap-kick. His lightning-fast foot would make contact before Tucker's gun even cleared its holster. Ki studied his opponent, and looked closely for the tensing of the jaw or the narrowing of the eyes that would signal Tucker's move.

Ki was ready when he saw Tucker's shoulder twitch, but he wasn't prepared for the shotgun he saw the bartender bring up to the level.

"Hold it!" the bartender commanded. "I'll have no killings in my saloon."

"Keep out of this," Tucker shot back angrily. "It ain't any of yer damned business."

"I'd hate to put any holes in my walls, Tucker. I reckon, though, your body'll stop most of the buckshot."

"You can order us around in here, Cooper, but not out there," Tucker said and shoved a shaking finger toward the door.

"You should be thanking me, Tucker. I just saved you from committing cold-blooded murder."

"The man called me out; you all heard it."

"Damn fool! Can't you see he's not wearing any guns?" For the first time, Tucker and the others looked down at Ki's waist, where they saw his black suit falling smoothly over his hips. "House rules say you buy the man a drink," the bartender said as he replaced the scattergun underneath the bar.

Tucker slapped a half-dollar on the bar, and Cooper passed him the bottle and two glasses. "We still don't know who shot up Hank," he muttered as he poured the drinks.

"Anyone here familiar with the Two Gun Kid?" Ki seized the opportunity to open up the subject of the outlaw.

Immediately Tucker slammed the bottle to the bar. "I think you just outlasted your welcome, Chinee. Get going."

From the corner of his eye Ki looked at the bartender.

23

There seemed to be no disagreement forthcoming. With a nod to the bartender, Ki left the saloon, and headed for his room at the hotel. He realized that this time he was the one who had broken one of the house rules. Apparently in the Silver Lode Saloon, where a breach of proper etiquette would cost a man a drink, one did not mention openly the name of the Two Gun Kid.

Chapter 3

While enjoying a large breakfast of ham steak, scrambled eggs, and warm biscuits, Ki told Jessie of his night in the saloon. "I don't think we'll find out much about the Two Gun Kid. People seem very hesitant to talk," he concluded finally.

Jessie put down her cup of coffee. "The fear of getting a bullet in the back will keep an awful lot of mouths closed," she agreed. "But there must be a few honest folks who aren't afraid to speak up."

"Trouble is, honest folk won't have much to tell us."

Jessie immediately understood what he was getting at. "I see what you mean, Ki, but if the law is afraid of the Two Gun Kid, and the sheriff can't get anyone to talk, how are we going to?"

"I've been wondering about that myself. Maybe the trick is to let the Two Gun Kid come to us."

"That won't prove he shot the marshal."

"No, but it's a start. The more we know about him, the

25

more we know about his motives, the easier it will be to find the proof."

Jessie nodded, but remained silent. Her face slowly turned sour. "Ki, what if there is no evidence?"

"There's always something that will lead us to the murderer."

"That's not what I mean," she said sullenly. "What if no one saw the Two Gun Kid come or go? What if he has a sound alibi?"

"We'll find the murderer," Ki repeated again with solid conviction.

"Ki," Jessie blurted out, "if we don't get any evidence, no court of law will convict the man."

"Does that matter?" Ki said softly.

Jessie didn't answer. Not because she didn't know the answer, but because she didn't like to admit it. The law—the legal, enforceable code of justice—went only so far. More often the "code of the West" reigned supreme. Frontier justice was famous, and although it was not always dispensed by the book, it was often swift and permanent. Frontier justice did more to tame the West than any marshal could ever do. In a land so vast, the law couldn't be everywhere. Jessie accepted that; it wouldn't be the first time she took matters into her own hands, but that didn't mean she liked it any better. When possible, she preferred to let the due process of law dispense justice.

"We're not in the middle of the prairie," she said almost to herself. "I think I'll go and have a talk with the sheriff." She pushed back her chair and rose to her feet.

"I wouldn't get your hopes too high," Ki advised.

"Maybe if he knows there are people, capable people, who'll stand by him he'll bring in the Two Gun Kid."

"Maybe. . . ."

Sheriff Boswell appeared to be the friendly and amiable sort. At least he was courteous. When Jessie entered his office he stood up from his desk, shook her hand warmly, and pulled out a chair for her. "Now what can I do for you, ma'am?"

Jessie studied the man who wore the tin star on his gray vest. He had a round, fleshy face, with wide-set dark eyes and a full head of thick, wavy, dark hair. He was once a good-looking man, but was now a few years past his prime. The fact that he was past forty surprised Jessie. For some reason, she had expected a younger man, but she didn't let her surprise show. "My name is Jessica Starbuck, and I'm a citizen who believes strongly in justice," she began cautiously.

"You've come to the right place, Miss Starbuck. Justice is my stock-in-trade." The sheriff smiled at her pleasantly but without much warmth. As Jessie thought about it, Boswell's age made more sense. In the sedate town of Coleville, the sheriff was more a political official meant to keep the town running smoothly than a hired gun who would have to tame outlaws and troublemakers. Most disputes could probably be judiciously settled without having to resort to firearms. A tactful, diplomatic man would probably serve as well if not better than a man with a lightning draw. A few years back it might have been different, but now the job was probably as cushiony as the sheriff's ample bottom.

Jessie decided to get right down to the point and lay her cards on the table. "I'm a Texas rancher with a fair amount of resources at my disposal," she said unabashedly.

The sheriff's smile remained painted on his face. "Ma'am, rich and mighty or poor and simple, you'll get equal treatment in this office."

Jessie ignored his comment and continued. "I was also a good friend of Marshal Dixon's."

"Marshal Dixon had lots of friends," he said cautiously, then changed his tone and added quickly, "An' I'm always glad to meet another."

"He also had one enemy."

"It was unfortunate," the sheriff said sympathetically.

27

"Yes, it was," Jessie agreed. "But it would be more unfortunate if the killer escaped unpunished."

"I assure you, Miss Starbuck, we're doing everything we can to find the killer." It was uncanny how the sheriff's pulpy lips remained fixed in the same smile.

"I don't suppose you have to look very far. The Two Gun Kid has been seen around town."

At the mention of the outlaw, Boswell's smile seemed to flicker, but he soon regained his composure. "Miss Starbuck, I'd be more than happy to engage you in idle gossip, perhaps tonight over dinner, but right now I have important business to attend to."

Jessie would not be dismissed so easily. "Sheriff, a cold-blooded murder has been committed in your town— the murder of not only a well-respected citizen, but an ex-lawman. I can't think of anything more important than apprehending the killer," she stated emphatically.

Boswell leaned forward in his chair. "Ma'am, I don't tell you how to run your herds, and I'd appreciate you not telling me how to run this town."

"Then I'm sure you don't need me to tell you of the rumors circulating in this town of yours," Jessie bluffed knowingly; there wasn't an elected official who wasn't concerned with his reputation.

"Look, Miss Starbuck, I'm doing everything I possibly can," he said in a more casual tone of voice. "I guarantee the killer will be brought to trial, but I refuse to go off half-cocked and arrest a man just because public opinion finds him guilty. As long as I'm sheriff in this town, circumstantial proof will not see a man hang. Now good day!"

Jessie had no other choice but to continue her investigation elsewhere. As she got up to leave she wondered if she had misjudged the man. Public opinion being what it was, perhaps it was true that even without sufficient evidence the Two Gun Kid would be found guilty of murder. Maybe Sheriff Boswell was not afraid of the Two Gun Kid, but was only trying to carry out his duties conscientiously. Maybe Boswell did not fear the guns of the outlaw, but wanted to make sure that overzealousness did not result in the hanging of the wrong man. Perhaps Sheriff Boswell was of that rare breed that really did believe a man was innocent until proven guilty.

Ki finished his breakfast, then stretched back in his chair and lingered over his second cup of coffee. Though Ki found no discomfort in hitting the trail before dawn, he was equally at home sitting and watching the sun creep slowly up in the sky. The trick was in knowing what to do when. There were situations when time was of the essence, then there were circumstances that were best served by letting events happen naturally. Repeatedly, Ki had come to find that being in the right place at the right time was often the secret to success. But one could never tell beforehand just where such a place might be found. It could be right here at the breakfast table, or it could be out on the street. And since there was no way to guess, there was also no reason to worry about it. With that thought in mind, Ki picked himself up and stepped out into the late-morning sunshine.

The town was already well into its working day. Coleville had originally sprung up as a mining town, but after the initial lode had petered out, many had stayed on and the town continued to prosper. Farmers began to homestead the southern end of the valley, while ranchers brought their herds to graze in the northern ranges. The two groups managed to coexist fairly peaceably; clear heads soon came to realize there was enough land for everybody. And in the mountains to the west, small prospectors continued to stake claims. Though there was no more mother lode, the small but steady finds of copper kept mining alive and lucrative. Coleville accommodated all three factions, growing to a nice size.

As Ki walked down the street the town seemed like any

29

of a dozen he had passed through before. The saloon, the bank, the livery, the general stores, the train and stage depots; he had seen the likes of them all elsewhere. But Coleville had two distinctions. One brought a smile to his face, the other caused him to grit his teeth in determination. A beautiful girl fresh out of finishing school would be out walking through fields of wildflowers while a fugitive murderer lurked somewhere in the shadows of town.

As Ki passed by the windows of the Silver Lode he saw a figure working behind the bar. On impulse, he backtracked and entered the saloon. "Morning," he said pleasantly.

"You're too early for a drink. Don't open till eleven," the bartender announced without looking up.

"It's not too early to say thanks, is it?" Ki said with a smile.

The bartender looked up and, seeing Ki, returned the smile. "Well, that all depends on what for—Mr. Ki, I believe it is."

Ki nodded. "No mister, just Ki. A common mistake," he added with a smile. "I'd like to thank you for intervening on my behalf last night."

The bartender extended his hand. "The name's Cooper, and you don't owe me anything."

Ki couldn't tell if that was his family name or given name, but it mattered little. He shook the hand. "I just want you to know I appreciate your standing up for me like that," Ki said sincerely. Though Ki felt the incident of the other night held little danger the bartender had no way of knowing that. Cooper had interceded on behalf of an apparently defenseless stranger. Ki respected him for that.

"I reckoned we owed you that much," Cooper stated plainly.

"Why is that?" Ki asked curiously.

"For bringing in Greene. These days too many folks don't want to get involved." Cooper continued to polish the bar as he talked. "Oh, they'd help an injured man all right. But a dead man's another thing."

Ki thought he knew what the bartender was getting at, but he wanted to draw the man out. "What do you mean?"

"You saw what happened here last night. People can get awfully suspicious. Sometimes it's easier to let a body just lie there than to do the decent thing. A man don't want to face too many questions, so he rides around the body and leaves it to the mext man, or the buzzards. Whichever comes first."

"An honest man shouldn't be afraid of a few questions," Ki said pointedly.

A slow smile crossed Cooper's face. "There ain't too many men that are that honest."

"Is that personal experience talking, or just good poker sense?"

"Maybe a little of both," Cooper answered sharply.

"And how do you think I stack up?" Ki asked.

The bartender studied him closely. "You might be one of those rare exceptions, Ki. Trouble is, a man can ask a few too many questions. Honest you may be, innocent you're not. But like I say, folks don't always see things clearly." Cooper turned to the rear wall and straightened the rows of liquor bottles.

"I owe you an apology, though I'm not sure why."

"Now that's something you don't hear often," the bartender said curiously.

"Seems like I offended quite a few people when I mentioned the Two Gun Kid," Ki said nonchalantly. "Yourself included," he added as an afterthought.

Cooper studied him carefully. "Ki, a little advice: you won't make many friends in this town by discussing Two Gun."

Ki noted immediately that Cooper had dropped the full title and referred to the outlaw in a more familiar fashion. "I'm not looking to make many friends," he said dryly.

31

"Then what exactly are you looking for?" There was no malice in the bartender's question, but neither was there much warmth.

"Some information, some answers."

"You won't get the same answer from any two men."

"I'm only asking you, Cooper. Most folks don't see things clearly," Ki added with a smile. "What is it about the Two Gun Kid that the mere mention of his name will get a man evicted from your saloon?"

Cooper placed his hands squarely on the bar and faced Ki. He hesitated, apparently considering how much to tell. "Being a stranger hereabouts I reckon you mean well," he began finally. "But there aren't many who don't know about the Two Gun Kid. Not that he's all that famous, like Jesse James or the Youngers, but unlike those others he did most of his riding in these parts. You never found him hightailing it up to Minnesota or the Dakotas. He spent all his time right around here."

"So people got to know him fairly well?" Ki surmised aloud.

The bartender nodded. "He's made a lot of friends and a lot of enemies over the years."

"But more enemies than friends?" Ki prompted.

"Depends on who you ask."

"I imagine people have some pretty strong feelings about him." The bartender nodded, and Ki continued. "So all in all it's best not to discuss the subject. Especially in places like gambling halls and saloons."

"You got it, Ki. He's a hero to some and a hellion to others." For a moment the case seemed closed, then Cooper seemed to reconsider and leaned closer to Ki. "You don't need to be packing irons to show your colors. Anyone who'll stand up to Tucker the way you did has got a whole lot of confidence and probably a heck of a lot more up his sleeve. Now I think I know what you want to hear, but you ain't going to hear it from me."

"Why is that?"

"'Cause whatever the Two Gun Kid might be, he ain't a cold-blooded murderer."

Ki thought that over in silence. He also wondered what mission the bartender suspected him to be on. He had not come to any conclusion when Cooper interrupted his thoughts.

"For some reason I've taken a liking to you, Ki. Don't know why, just have."

"I appreciate it, Cooper. Good friends are hard to come by."

"So I'd hate to see you go stickin' yer nose in a gopher hole and get yer ass shot off."

Jessie walked out of Olsen's General Store with a troubled look on her face. It was her first stop. She didn't really need the few sundries she ordered; she did need information. She had seen the proprietor at the cemetery, and his store seemed as good a place as any to start. As the friendly Mr. Olsen totaled up her purchases, Jessie casually made mention of the funeral service. "The minister had some fine things to say about Marshal Dixon."

Olsen nodded. "Eugene was a good man. We'll all miss him dearly."

"I reckon the sheriff'll turn this town upside-down trying to find the killer."

The proprietor pushed back his spectacles. "Sheriff Boswell?"

Jessie nodded. "I thought he was conducting an investigation."

That brought a chuckle from the storekeeper. "There's no need for an investigation, ma'am. We all know who shot Eugene."

Jessie wanted to ask why no one was doing anything about it, but instead she paid for her purchases.

"Thank you, ma'am," Olsen said as he handed her her change.

Her next stop was the dressmaker's. Again, her conversation with the kindly Mrs. Benson confirmed two things. The Two Gun Kid was believed to be the murderer, and the sheriff was doing nothing about it. But both Mr. Olsen and Mrs. Benson were friends of the Dixons. Perhaps if she talked to someone else she would get a different story. Jessie turned toward the stable.

It was only natural to ask about her team and rig. But when she first inquired about them the elderly stable manager didn't seem to place her. He squinted his eyes, then his cracked face broke out into a toothless smile. "Sorry I didn't recognize you, Miss Starbuck. You're dressed a mite different."

Jessie couldn't resist a smile. In her tight denim jeans, polished leather boots, and loose-fitting silk blouse she cut quite a different figure from the day before. Despite his age, the man still seemed to appreciate her physical virtues. "I don't dress for a funeral every day, Mr. . . . ?" she said engagingly.

"Jus' call me Wes."

"All right, Wes. You seem to board a lot of animals here."

Wes nodded. "We take good care of 'em."

Jessie proceeded to make small talk with the stable manager. His admiration of her seemed to grow as he discovered she could talk horses with the best of them. Now that they were on more friendly terms and a first-name basis Jessie decided to start digging for information. "You've lived here most your life, Wes?" she asked pleasantly.

"All my life, Jessie," he informed her.

"Then you knew Marshal Dixon?"

Wes nodded. "An' I know what yer thinkin', too. Why weren't I at the buryin'? An' I'll tell you, Jessie. 'Cause I seen too many buryin's in my days. Don't have the stomach for 'em anymore."

"I wasn't wondering about that at all," Jessie told him kindly. "I can certainly understand the way you feel, Wes."

The old man smiled weakly. "You can?" he asked with

34

surprise. Jessie nodded. "Trouble is," Wes began as he scratched at his gray whiskers, "I can't figure why the young ones always go first and leave the old ones like me behind."

"Because I think you've still got a drink or two due you yet," she said with a smile.

"Wisdom from the mouth of babes," West cackled as he slapped his knees.

Jessie didn't think there'd ever be a good opening, so she jumped right in. "Wes, how about the Two Gun Kid, know him too?"

A slow smile crossed his face. "I c'n remember when the Kid really was a kid," he said as he reached for a broom. "Used to come riding through here with his pa."

"Most people seemed to think he killed Marshal Dixon."

"They're entitled to their opinions."

"But you don't think so?" she asked boldly.

Wes leaned heavily on the broomstick. "I ain't in any position to know," he said cagily.

Jessie thought that over in her head. "Wes, why is it that anyone who knows anything about the Two Gun Kid won't talk, and everyone who doesn't know him is ready to hang him?" she asked openly.

"Maybe 'cause those that know him like him," he answered plainly.

"You don't find many respectable people liking outlaws."

"Let's jus' say there's respectable and then there's *respectable.*"

"Wes, if you're trying to tell me that—"

"Jessie, there've been many folks here that have cussed the bank, the railroads, and the large ranchers with all the breath they have. Good folks that've been run off their land for one reason or another. All legal and proper, but wrong jus' the same. Now when someone like the Kid fights back you're gonna get a lot of folks to stand right behind him.

Maybe not out in public, but deep down in here." He tapped his finger to his heart.

"I hope I'm not prying, Wes, but you sound like you might be one of them."

"Damn straight I am!" he snapped proudly.

"Any particular reason?"

The old man nodded. "I weren't always a stable hand, Jessie. I used to own the first livery here in Coleville. Right down on the other side of Main Street. But that was before Randolph Hollowell decided it was time for him to get into the livery trade."

Jessie knew the scenario well. "And there wasn't room for two stables," she said knowingly. It wasn't a question.

"Care to take a guess which one survived?" Wes said bitterly.

Jessie shook her head no. She would have liked to have asked more about this Hollowell character, but she didn't want to stir up more bitter feelings.

Wes seemed to recover quickly, though. "But a man's gotta eat, an' I was too old for anything but respectable work . . ."

"You mean you were too old to be out robbing banks and trains," Jessie said with a smile. Wes nodded. "But we're not talking about simple robbery, Wes. We're talking cold-blooded murder!"

"Poppycock! The Kid ain't no murderer. Least he weren't before they locked him up."

"What do you mean by that, Wes?" Jessie wondered aloud.

"Prison can turn a man ugly!" Just then a trim buggy driven by a tall, dapper gentleman rolled into the stable. "Excuse me, Jessie."

"Thanks for the talk, Wes," Jessie said sincerely.

"It was a pleasure speakin' with you," he said over his shoulder as he went to grab hold of the horse's bit.

Jessie wasn't certain, but she thought she heard Wes address the man as Mr. Hollowell.

• • •

Having nothing better to do, and needing some time to think things over, Jessie headed back to her hotel room. As she came up the stairs she thought she saw the figure of a man climb through the hallway's rear window. Preoccupied as she was, she didn't think anything of it until she opened her door. Her room was a mess. Someone—and it didn't take much to suspect the fleeing stranger—had totally ransacked her room.

Chapter 4

Jessie burst into the Silver Lode Saloon gasping for breath. At the sound of her footsteps Ki turned around immediately. "Jessie!" he exclaimed. "Are you all right?" he asked worriedly.

Jessie nodded her head. "Someone broke into my room ...I chased him into the alley...but he's gone." Her words came out between breaths.

"Stay here," Ki ordered as he raced to the door.

"He's gone, Ki," Jessie repeated emphatically. She pulled a chair out from one of the tables and slumped down into it.

Ki stuck his head out into the street and looked both ways before he came back and sat down next to her. "What happened?" he asked.

"I was going back to my room when I saw a man step out the hallway window." She had regained her breath and her voice was once again calm and relaxed. "I didn't think anything of it until I entered my room and saw it had been searched. I ran back out into the hall; the window opened up over the back alley. By the time I got outside there was no trace of the man. He could have slipped out between any of the other buildings."

"There probably was a horse tethered nearby," Ki guessed out loud.

Jessie nodded. "I looked for tracks."

"Did you find any?"

"About two dozen," she said with a smile.

"A silly question," Ki admitted quickly.

"I'd like to know if he searched your room too," Jessie wondered.

"We can find out easy enough. But there's no rush. First, I'd like you to meet a friend of mine." He turned to introduce Jessie to Cooper, but the bar was vacant and the man was nowhere to be seen.

Back at the hotel, they soon found out that Ki's room had also been hit. His mattress was flipped onto the floor and dresser drawers were thrown all over the place. Ki had few personal belongings, but his new suit lay crumpled in the corner. "If my room was untouched I might have considered it to be a case of mistaken identity. Our visitor just might have had the wrong room."

"I even thought it might be nothing more than a simple robbery—"

"But?"

"But he found my Colt, and left it on the bed."

Ki thought that over. Jessie's custom-made Colt would fetch a handsome price or make a prized addition to any collection. It would also prove useful and practical to anyone in the habit of breaking into other people's rooms.

"All this mess is depressing," Jessie announced. "Let's go down and have an early supper."

"Fine with me," Ki agreed as he stepped over a drawer and followed Jessie into the hall. But as he closed the door he changed his mind. "On second thought, Jessie, why don't you go on without me. I'll join you in a few minutes.

The thought of my new suit lying on the floor—"

"Ki, I knew it was odd when you first bought that suit, but this sudden concern with neatness—"

"Jessie, it would not have been proper to let you go to the funeral in a new dress and have me in my old worn clothes," Ki explained patiently. "I was only showing my respects for Mrs. Dixon and her family."

"To think you'd refuse to escort me into the dining room just to get a few wrinkles out of your clothes—why, it's almost vain," she said with a piercing smile. Ki shrugged sheepishly. Jessie turned and headed down the steps, muttering to herself, "And all this from a man who'd wear the same shirt for a month of Sundays. . . ."

The moment her back was turned, Ki's coy smile vanished. There was one thing he had to check and he didn't want to alarm her needlessly. When she was safely out of sight he raced to her room and entered it silently.

He picked her Colt up from the bed and cracked open its cylinder. In the chamber were six cartridges—just as there should be. He took a deep breath and relaxed.

There couldn't be a more fatal mistake than to go into a showdown with an unloaded gun. It would be the mark of a shrewd adversary to secretively unload one's gun, then later force you into a situation where you had to rely on that very same, but now useless, weapon.

Ki headed down to the dining room somewhat relieved yet still perplexed as to the identity and purpose of the intruder. As soon as he sat down Jessie began to speak. "Could it have been your friend Tucker?" she asked enthusiastically without any preface.

"I thought of him too, but he wouldn't have known we were traveling together," Ki answered.

"I'd really like to know who that man was," Jessie puzzled aloud.

"More important is why he did what he did," Ki added.

"When we know *who,* we'll know why," Jessie countered.

40

Ki remained firm. "When we know *why*, we'll know who."

Jessie smiled curtly, but Ki already knew she was annoyed. "You do it your way, and I'll do it my way," she said peevishly.

"Fine," Ki said with a scowl. Instantly they both broke out into laughter. "Who knew we were traveling together?" Ki asked with a genuine smile.

"Besides the hotel staff, everyone at the funeral." She thought it over briefly. "That's not much help, is it?"

"It's a start."

"All right. Then who would break in and leave my Colt behind?" Jessie asked Ki.

"Someone who had no use for it," he answered simply. "Someone who had no need for either money or guns," he elaborated after a moment.

"Someone who could rob a bank at will and had all the guns he could use. Well, at least two. . . ."

They said it almost simultaneously: "The Two Gun Kid!"

"And just when I was beginning to like the man, too," Jessie muttered under her breath.

"You sound almost dejected," Ki noted with a smirk. "You're not annoyed that my methods proved more fruitful?"

"Just confused, Ki. I heard a few things today that made me doubt the Two Gun Kid was our man, but once again everything seems to point to his guilt."

Ki smiled understandingly. "If it's any consolation, Jessie, I'm as confused as you, if not more so. I can't decide on what to eat." It was true that Ki was confused, but it wasn't over the dinner selection. His levity only concealed his concern over the timely disappearance of Cooper back at the Silver Lode Saloon.

Jessie moved easily in the saddle as her chestnut mare galloped down the trail. When she looked back and realized

Ki's brown gelding wouldn't catch her, she slowed her mount to a walk. In the evening twilight the entire landscape became a soft, muted gray-green. Grass, trees, and sky were practically indistinguishable. The first stars were not yet visible, but the crickets and frogs were already active and vocal. The meadow they rode through was full of the chirping insects, but they always seemed louder off in the near distance. Jessie would focus in on the *wibbit* of a tree frog, then smile to herself as the creature turned silent as she rode by, only to start up again once she passed. She closed her eyes and let the sounds surround her. The falling of her mare's hooves kept a steady beat for the melodies of the crickets and frogs. She only opened her eyes when she heard Ki's horse approach.

"You're going to laugh, Ki, but on a night like this I miss the soft bellow of cattle."

"Spoken like a true rancher," he said with a grin. "It's the heart of the Starbuck empire."

Jessie seemed offended. "I wasn't thinking in monetary terms, Ki."

"I know you better than that, Jessie. It's your love for ranching that makes it work. Even those big Kansas City-owned combines don't run as profitably or as smoothly as the Circle Star."

Jessie accepted what was, in fact, the truth. "You can take my mines, lumber mills, packing houses, and shipping companies, and just leave me with a few hundred head and I'd be happy."

"I believe you would be, Jessie."

"That's what bothers me the most. With all the land, good land, still available, I don't see why men have to turn to stealing and robbing. There's still so much you can get the honest way," she said with a sigh. Before Ki could answer she turned to him with a sly smile. "Of course I do understand the blacker side, but sometimes, when I'm listening to the crickets, I like to pretend I don't."

"Innocence has its place, Jessie, but in the real world

nothing takes the place of knowledge."

Jessie nodded and smiled. "And I don't think there's a cowhand around who knows half of what you do, Ki," she teased playfully, but inside she truly believed it.

"At least not within a good ten miles," he agreed.

They rode a ways in silence as night crept up on them quickly. It was under the cloak of darkness that Jessie first spotted the rider on the ridge to their left. "Ki, how long has that rider been tailing us?" she asked. She knew it was unnecessary to point out his presence to Ki. If she knew he was there, so did Ki.

"I first spotted him before we broke into a trot. But then I wasn't sure he was following us."

"That's why you suggested a run?"

Ki nodded. "There's no doubt now. He's not only going our way, he's keeping our pace."

"Maybe you should try to double back behind him?" Jessie suggested.

"I have a feeling he knows the terrain quite well, and he certainly has his eyes on us. I don't think there's much hope of catching him off guard."

"You could slip off your horse, and I'd bunch the two animals together. At this distance and in the dark he may not notice. If I keep to a slow walk, that would give you time enough to circle around."

Ki seemed pleased with her. "That might work," he said, thinking it over. "But I'm not sure what it would accomplish."

"It would—" Jessie started, then stopped short. "I see what you mean."

"Remember we're looking for proof, not suspects. We need evidence that he's a murderer, not that he's been following us."

"I guess you're right, Ki. But just the same, I'd feel better if we lost him."

"Any time you're ready."

It was a simple matter to lose the rider. Jessie waited till he had dipped down below the ridge, then she spurred her horse off to the left. Once behind a dense row of thickets and hidden from prying eyes, they continued on a perpendicular course. Over the next knoll Jessie and Ki described a large circle to ultimately approach their destination—the Dixon house—from the totally opposite direction.

The house was in sight when Ki turned to Jessie. "Something's been bothering me, Jessie—I think we might have made a mistake."

"How so?"

"This ride brought Greene—the man we found dead—back to mind. I didn't think about it at first because I was so wrapped up with Marshal Dixon and the Two Gun Kid, but now I think it's rather strange a two-bit stable hand gets bushwhacked for no apparent reason."

"It's happened before. There's always someone with a score to settle," Jessie pointed out.

"That's possible. But we never gave it much thought. I even told myself I was after the marshal's killer, not Greene's. If they proved to be one and the same, fine—"

"What are you getting at, Ki?" Jessie said a bit impatiently.

"I'm not quite certain, Jessie. But I'm starting to ask myself a few questions. Like what was Greene doing out here? From what I heard he wasn't the sort to take a relaxing evening ride."

"Ki, there are any number of things he might have been doing."

"I know. But I keep wondering if he was heading just where we are when a rider shot at him from the ridge."

Jessie saw his point immediately, but she had no comment. Just then Ki pointed to his right, to the same ridge that ran the length of the valley. "Jessie, up there, quick!"

She turned just in time to catch the silhouette of a horse and rider before they vanished behind a rocky outcropping. "He must have known where we were heading," she said with a start.

★

Chapter 16

Two Gun didn't have to turn around to recognize the voice. "There's no call for that, Tucker. I won't try anything," he said as he raised his hands slowly.

Tucker stood high on a boulder that was behind them and to their left. A 12-bore shotgun was aimed in the general vicinity of Jessie's head. He let out a laugh. "I don't see as how you have a choice."

"Let the girl go, Tucker. You got no business with her, " he said as he turned cautiously in the saddle.

Again, Tucker laughed crudely. "Ooee! Do I got business with her. I'm gonna give her some learnin' on what a real man is."

"Let her go, Tucker." The Kid sounded desperate.

"I'm gonna drill her with my prod so many times she won't be able to walk. . . ."

"Let her go, and I'll forget this happened," Two Gun said appeasingly.

"It'll be a sight to see, Kid. Too bad you won't get the chance. Yer lids'll be staring at the devil. . . ."

"Tucker. Don't be a fool. I got no quarrel with you—yet."

"That's not how I see it."

"Your brother was a good man, Tucker. When he rode with me he knew the risks."

"My brother was a fool. And that's why he's dead. Jimmy should have never thrown in with a two-bit slinger like you. I'm twice the man you are, Kid."

"Your brother was my friend, Tucker," the Kid said sadly. "There's no bad blood between us."

"Even if I was the one who sent the law in after you?"

"You!"

"That's right, Kid. Jimmy was so full of you he couldn't keep his mouth shut."

"But—"

"I knew the job you were pulling."

"But before the marshal caught up to me, the posse shot Jimmy. You just about killed your own brother!"

Tucker shrugged. "Hollowell was paying good money."

Jessie could see the pain and anger in Two Gun's face.

"But that's not all. I killed 'bout as many men as the famed Two Gun Kid," Tucker boasted. "I laid the marshal in his grave, and Greene, and—"

"You lousy, stinkin' bastard!" Only the fact that Jessie would get hurt kept him from going for his guns. He was so full of rage he cared nothing about his own safety.

"I knew you were coming for me. Hollowell was right. Either I plug you first, or. . . . And Greene knew I was gunning for you. I reckon he got the suspicion that I had killed the marshal by mistake. When I saw him ridin' out to the Dixon spread, I plugged him, too. But I'm through talkin'. Now I'm gonna become the man that killed the Two Gun Kid."

"Wait!" Jessie cried. "I wish you were as smart as you were brave, Tucker."

"What's that mean, bitch?"

176

"I know where his money is. Kill the Kid and we'll be partners."

"Hear that, Kid? She's double-crossing you." Tucker seemed joyous at the prospect of further insulting his rival. "You're gonna die with the taste of it in yer mouth."

"You *are* a fool, Tucker," Jessie said calmly. "What are they going to say when they see the Kid full of buckshot? Are they going to talk about how Tucker outdrew him? How Tucker is the faster draw? Are they going to call you the better man, Tucker? Uh-uh. They're going to say how Tucker hid behind a rock and had to waylay the Kid with a scattergun. They'll laugh in your face."

"Shut up! No one laughs in my face."

"Then they'll laugh behind your back, Tucker. But do it the right way and they'll look up to you. They'll call you the best."

"What are you talking about?" Tucker's interest was raised.

"Look at him, Tucker. You shot him up pretty bad in the alley. He can't use but one arm. Pump him full of bullets and you'll be a hero. Let him die with a gun in his hand, and everyone will know who the fastest draw is."

"You little skunk," Two Gun snapped at Jessie.

"Shut up, Kid!" Tucker warned. "The lady's talkin' horse sense."

"She's a tramp, Tucker, an' she'll do to you what she did to me."

"You going to let him call your woman that?" Jessie said demurely. The remark seemed to please Tucker. "It'd make a gal proud to belong to the man who outdrew the famous Two Gun Kid."

"Listen to her and you'll dig your own grave," the Kid said frantically. "No one'll ever believe you could outdraw me!"

"Show him, Tucker," Jessie urged.

"Even with my bad shoulder I'll pump you full of lead,"

Two Gun continued to taunt.

"Show him who's the best," Jessie cried fervently.

A slow smile crossed Tucker's face. His eyes twinkled. "Get down," he ordered Jessie. As she dismounted Tucker saw the Colt that was hugging her hip. "Now drop that gun, lady."

Jessie's heart sank. The minute Tucker turned to face the Kid she had planned to draw on him, but she did as she was told. If Tucker gave Two Gun an honest chance there was probably little to worry about. But that was an awfully big "if."

Tucker turned to the outlaw. "Now you, Kid, but keep yer hands high." Two Gun slipped his feet from the stirrups, swung a leg over the saddlehorn, and slid down. "Now drop yer right gun. Anythin' more than two fingers touch that gun and you'll be deprivin' me of a lot of pleasure."

"You crawlin' coward. . . ."

Tucker laughed heartily. "You still got yer one gun."

"My left! You call that a fair draw?"

Two Gun said it so convincingly that even Jessie began to worry. But the Kid dropped his gun as ordered and shook his left arm to loosen it and help get back the circulation.

Tucker smiled. "I've waited a long time for this," he said almost to himself. Very carefully he lowered the shotgun to the rock. The smile stayed glued to his face. "All right, Kid. When you get tired of livin', slap leather. . . ."

Ki and Cooper heard the crack of the six shots. They reared their horses around and took off at a gallop.

It happened quickly. Two Gun's hand moved in a blur. His gun came up, spitting fire. The first shot caught Tucker in the chest. The second bullet knocked the man off his feet. Faceup, Tucker started to slide down the front of the and Luke Hollowell, still clutching his Winchester rifle, fell to the floor, dead.

He stared at the body. Silent, unmoving. Then after a long, long, moment he turned and walked down the steps. Suddenly, he was sickened by the stink of greed that permeated the house.

Jessie could see the mansion when she heard the shots. An unrealistic fear gripped her and she pushed her horse even faster. The fear grew as the seconds passed and no one emerged from the building.

She slowed her horse to a walk. The tears in her eyes obstructed her vision. She didn't immediately see the figure step down from the porch. But she did see the second figure that stepped into the doorway. And she saw the barrel of the rifle that was just now being leveled. . . .

"Behind you!" she screamed as loud as possible.

Two Gun turned slowly, as if he no longer felt the need for haste. He saw the shotgun that was pointing directly at him. Very deliberately, he aimed his sixgun and fired. It took the briefest part of a second.

The shotgun crashed to the floor. Old Man Hollowell grabbed his wounded forearm. Then, shocked and grief-stricken, he collapsed on the porch.

The Two Gun Kid walked out of the yard, closed the gate behind him, and continued walking.

Jessie caught up with him on the road and swung down from the saddle beside him.

"There weren't no mercy in it, Jessie," he said soberly. "There's no kindness in a father burying his son. . . ." Then he turned and continued walking.

Jessie said nothing but followed in step. A few minutes later they came to the tree where Two Gun had his horse tethered.

He turned to her, searching for the words.

"Don't say anything, just hold me," Jessie said softly.

The Kid took her in his arms and held her tight. When they separated, she was looking at a different man.

Two Gun pulled out the Colt Peacemaker from his right holster and handed it to Jessie. "I want you to have this."

"Two Gun . . ."

"I don't need it; the Two Gun Kid is finished."

"What will you do? Where will you go?"

The Kid shrugged. "Someplace far away. Up north—Montana. Maybe try my hand at ranchin'."

"Ranching?" she said with a laugh. Jessie didn't mean it to come out that way, but the thought of the Kid, the best gunslinger she had ever seen, herding cattle, made her laugh.

Surprisingly, Two Gun laughed with her. "There are lots of things I can do well," he said with a grin.

Jessie didn't care that he was poking fun at her. "I remember," she said with a twinkle in her eye.

"Besides that," he said with mock annoyance, "I can use a rope as good as I can a six-shooter. Well, almost. I can only lasso with my left."

"You'll make a damned good rancher," Jessie said firmly. "When you get settled, send a cable and I'll ship you some gen-u-ine Texas longhorns."

"Once I get a place, I might just do that," the Kid said sincerely. "But only if'n you come up with 'em."

"Just for a visit."

"Just for a visit," the Kid agreed. There was an uncomfortable pause, then Two Gun took hold of the horse's reins. "I best be movin' on now. . . ."

"I'll be waiting for that cable," Jessie said with a touch of sorrow.

"It'll come," Two Gun promised, "signed Delbert."

"I'll be looking forward to it, Mr. Fenster." Then, with a tear running down her cheek, she kissed the Two Gun Kid good-bye. Forever.

45

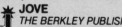

boulder. That was when the other four bullets slammed into the man's face. At the foot of the rock, Tucker slumped into a lifeless heap. Down the face of the granite a bright-red streak of blood marked the path of the body; four distinct patches of pink marked the spots where pieces of Tucker's brain were splattered against the rock.

Jessie ran to Two Gun and embraced him tightly. "That was the first man I ever enjoyed killing," he said soberly. "But it won't be the last," he added under his breath.

"You had no choice."

"I didn't have to like it."

"You're only human, Delbert."

The sound of his real name relaxed the Kid. "I'm just grateful you weren't hurt."

"I was so afraid," Jessie admitted openly. "Especially when you had to draw with your left."

Two Gun pulled himself away from Jessie. His face wore a huge pie-eating grin as he proceeded to twirl his revolver around his left trigger finger. He kept it spinning and, as he flamboyantly replaced the gun in its holster, announced simply, "I'm a lefty."

Out of the corner of his eye, Two Gun saw the two riders approaching. He took Jessie in his arms, kissed her passionately, then grabbed his horse's reins and hurried across the boulder field.

Jessie bent down to pick up her gun and noticed that even in his haste Two Gun had managed to retrieve his other Peacemaker. She wanted to rush after the Kid, but she knew where he was going. Maybe she should have tried to change his mind, but she wasn't sure she really wanted to.

Maybe the Kid was right. Maybe there *was* only one "real law." And the Two Gun Kid was as good at dispensing frontier justice as any man living.

The Hollowell mansion stood awesome against the darkening twilight sky. But the lone man standing in its shadow refused to be intimidated by its flagrant display of wealth and power.

"Hollowell!" he screamed loudly, perhaps even louder than was necessary. "Hollowell, come on out, or I'm coming in." He didn't wait for a response. He strode up to the large French windows that opened onto the porch, kicked in the glass, and stepped through the white lace curtains.

"I'm going to give you a chance, Hollowell. That's more than you gave my father. . . ."

There was the sound of feet scampering and doors closing quickly—servants getting out of the way, running to safety.

He walked through the empty parlor, ignoring the lush appointments, the likes of which he had never seen, nor would ever see again. He stepped cautiously into the hall, then into the dining room. He kicked open the door of the kitchen, stepping through quickly. The room, the entire floor, was deserted.

He looked up the wide central staircase and began his slow ascent. He walked softly and carefully. They would be waiting for him upstairs. Hiding behind a door, or under a bed. But they would be waiting, gun in hand.

He slipped both guns from their holsters, feeling the Peacemakers' solid weight in his hands, drawing strength from the accustomed feel of the smooth wood handles.

The step under him groaned as he shifted his leg. It didn't matter; they knew he was coming.

He gained the landing and turned the knob of the first door. As it swung open, he sensed as much as heard the faint creak of a door opening behind him.

Reeling on his heels, he fired two shots, one from each sixgun.

The first bullet splintered the edge of a closet door. The second bullet bloodied it as it struck a human skull.

Against the weight of the body, the door swung open,

"And it's almost as if he wants us to know it, too!" Ki's words sent a shiver up her back.

They were just yards from the house when Jessie eased her horse close to Ki's. "Ki, before we go in, there's something I want to say." She spoke in a hushed voice. "This ride got me to thinking, too."

"About?"

"The Two Gun Kid. If he came to gun down the marshal, why is he still sticking around? Once they laid Eugene in the ground he should have hightailed it out of here. Why didn't he?"

"It's a good question, Jessie. Maybe we can get some answers from Nell."

As it turned out they didn't get any answers from Nell. What they did get was some very good home-baked elderberry pie. Nell whisked them into the kitchen where the smell of the fresh-baked pie filled the room. Katie was just setting the pie on the table when she saw Ki. She looked like she was about to rush into his arms, but she restrained herself, saying rather calmly, "Why Jessie, Ki, what a pleasant surprise. I was going to bring you this pie tomorrow. But this is so much better," she added sweetly.

"We decided to bake some for all our friends, a thank-you for their support," Nell explained. "You'll get the first. Now, sit down."

"You seem well," Jessie commented.

Nell nodded. "Eugene's gone. No amount of grievin'll change that. And we ain't likely to forget him, either." She went over and put her arm around her daughter's waist, pulling her close. "So we decided to get on with it." She forced herself into a smile. "So from here on out, we'll have no more sorrow, no more tears, and no more talk about what could've or should've been!"

"I'm glad to hear it," Jessie said supportively, but as Nell turned to fetch them plates, Jessie and Ki exchanged a frustrated glance. After Nell's pronouncement, Jessie just didn't have the heart to quiz the woman about her husband

and his affairs with the Two Gun Kid.

Ki seemed to read her thoughts. "Don't worry, Jessie," he said in a soft voice. "We'll get the answers somewhere else."

"What was that, Ki?" Nell asked.

"I was just telling Jessie, next to gooseberry, elderberry pie is my favorite," Ki countered quickly.

"Then count your blessings, mister," Katie piped in happily. "This here's got 'em both. Eat up." Nell set down the plates, and Katie filled them with thick, steaming wedges of pie.

Jessie took a bite and savored the taste. "My compliments to the chefs, ladies. A woman could grow fat and not even give a hoot, eating these."

"Why, thank you, Jessie," Nell said. "But I don't think there's much danger of you fattening up much."

"With baking like this, though, you never can tell."

"How about you, Ki? We haven't heard what you think —" Katie stopped as she turned towards him, realizing why he had said nothing.

Ki lifted his empty plate. "If it's no trouble, ma'am, I wouldn't mind another piece," he said boyishly.

"I reckon that's the nicest compliment one could ask for," Katie said as she dished him out another slice. "Daddy used to say he could—" She stopped short and looked nervously at her mother.

"It's all right, Katie. Reckon there's no sense hiding the happy memories either." Nell finished her daughter's statement for her. "Gene used to say he could eat the whole blasted thing himself." She turned to Ki and looked him over approvingly. "It's nice to have a hearty appetite around the place again."

"Well, now that you mention it," Ki began, "we don't have our saddlebags with us, and there's no good way to pack half a pie."

Jessie agreed. "Reckon it won't travel too well on your lap either," she said with mock seriousness.

Ki shook his head. "Nope."

"I reckon it'll do a lot better in his stomach," Katie said with equal seriousness. "Might as well finish it, Ki."

Ki passed his plate to Katie. "Don't mind if I do, ma'am," he said with a toothy, berry-coated smile.

When the eating was done, Katie cleared the plates, and Nell turned to Jessie. "Now what brings you out this way?" she asked.

"We decided to go out for a ride. Town was getting hot and stuffy," she explained. "Once we were on the road, Ki suggested we stop in to see how you were making out."

Ki looked a bit surprised. That wasn't exactly how it happened. It was Jessie's idea to ride out and question Nell further about the Two Gun Kid. But then Katie turned around and exclaimed, "That's awfully nice of you, Ki," and he began to understand Jessie's manipulation of the truth.

"You'll be spending the night." The way Nell spoke it was not a question. "Go and get the extra blankets, Katie." Katie's eyes twinkled as she turned to leave.

"I'm afraid I can't, Nell. I have to meet someone at the Silver Lode," Ki said.

Katie stopped in her tracks. "Oh?" she said with raised eyebrows.

Obviously she knew of the saloon's reputation. Ki found himself blushing, but then Jessie came to the rescue.

"That man you wanted me to meet earlier, what was his name, Ki?"

"Cooper." Though Katie seemed to accept that better, she still seemed disappointed.

"That's right." Jessie turned to the older woman. "Nell, we'll take you up on your hospitality another night," she said apologetically, then got up from her chair.

"Come out early in the evening an' we'll have more'n a pie for you."

"You bet," Katie added with the quickest and cutest wink Ki had ever seen.

• • •

The ride back to town was quick and uneventful, and they saw no trace of their mysterious rider. They left their horses at the stable and started to walk down the quiet main street to the hotel. "Were you really planning on meeting Cooper at the saloon," Jessie finally asked, "or was that a convenient excuse?"

"Why would I need an excuse?"

"Don't play innocent with me, Ki. I saw the way Katie was eyeing you."

"I hadn't noticed," he said, pretending naïveté. "But if I had, I might have reconsidered."

"I don't know why I ever bring up the subject," Jessie said with self-reproach.

"I am going to the saloon." Ki was all seriousness. "I'd like to discuss a few things with Cooper. I have a feeling he knows more than he's letting on."

That sparked Jessie's interest. "What makes you say that?"

"For one, there was his disappearance earlier this afternoon. I think he's rather well acquainted with the Two Gun Kid."

"Wes also seemed rather fond of the Kid. I wonder..."

They had just stepped off the boardwalk when a voice came out of the shadows. "I hear he's a likable sort...." Jessie froze. It wasn't the words that caused the reaction, it was the unmistakable click of a revolver's hammer being cocked back. Apparently their assailant noticed her tense up, too. "It's always good to deal with other professionals," the voice said cryptically. "I can see there's no need to tell you what's pointed right at your backs," the man continued in a calm, steady voice. "Just step back into the alley real easy-like, and keep your hands up where I can see 'em."

★

Chapter 5

Ki did just as he was told. He would never risk doing anything that might endanger Jessie's life. Besides, if their assailant had intended to shoot them they would already be lying in a pool of blood.

Jessie also backed up into the recesses of the alley. She kept her hands up high, but slowly turned around. She couldn't get a clear look at the man; the moon, still low in the sky, shed no light into the alley. But there was no mistaking the two silver gun barrels that were pointed right at them. "The Two Gun Kid!" she practically gasped.

"At your service," the Kid said engagingly. But there was nothing charming about his two sixguns. Ki turned around. "Easy, Ki. Don't try anything foolish." Jessie was shocked that the outlaw knew his name, but Ki didn't seem surprised in the least.

"I won't," Ki assured him flatly.

The outlaw took a deep breath and relaxed his tense guard. "The hunters become the hunted—poetic justice," he postulated freely. Even in the dark his eyes seemed to twinkle.

"What do you know about justice?" Jessie snapped.

"I spent enough years in prison to know all about it." There was little rancor in his words. "What do *you* know about justice?" he continued. "No more than you have to, and no more than it pays."

"We know all about shooting lawmen in the back—" Jessie began hotly.

The Kid cut her off sharply. "You're on the wrong side of these six-shooters to be mouthing off like that!"

But Jessie was not to be silenced. "You can't shoot your way out of everything," she said defiantly.

The Two Gun Kid's tone softened. "Another time, another place, I'd be willing to discuss that at length with you, ma'am. But you'll be leaving town shortly. Say your farewells, pay your bills, and hit the road." Jessie had been threatened and run out of town many a time, but never with as much patient consideration as now.

She started to speak and the outlaw interrupted her again. "I ain't got no more time for any lousy, stinkin' bounty hunters. You can leave tomorrow, straight in the saddle, or day-after-next, belly down!"

Jessie and Ki exchanged looks. Apparently the outlaw thought they were bounty hunters after him for the money. "You're all wrong about that," she started to say, but her words were cut short.

Suddenly, from the rear of the alley came two loud cracks. Blue streaks of light cut through the night. Gunshots! The Kid reeled around. There was the pounding of a fleeing horse. The outlaw took one step in pursuit, then crumpled into the dirt.

Jessie and Ki rushed to the fallen body. "He's still alive," Jessie said hurriedly.

Ki needed no other word before taking off in pursuit of the gunman. He raced down the alley and out of sight.

Jessie turned her full attention to the outlaw. The Two

50

Gun Kid's breathing was labored, his eyes open but staring off into the distance. "I think you're going to be all right," she assured him softly, as much for her own sake as for his. The outlaw did not answer.

She studied his body, looking for his wounds. At first she did not see any, then she realized he would be shot in the back and gently eased him to his side. As she put her arms under him her fingers found a warm, wet, sticky spot. The outlaw groaned in pain, and Jessie eased him back down gently. With a little light she could get a better sense of the bullet hole. She pulled out a match and struck it against the bottom of her boot. The sulfur flared to life, and Jessie let out a horrified gasp. The entire right side of the Two Gun Kid's face was covered with blood.

The match burned out against her fingers, but Jessie hardly noticed it. She pulled out her shirttail and started to dab at the blood, but it continued to flow faster than she could clean it up. She had the sickening feeling that she was attempting to mop up the back side of his face from the front. He had been shot from behind; the bullet would have entered from the back. But she knew that couldn't be. If the Kid were shot in the head he wouldn't be breathing now. From the distance he was shot, a .44-caliber slug would have taken with it a large part of the outlaw's brain. She was just getting that gruesome picture from her mind when Ki returned.

"How is he?" he asked as he dropped down to one knee.

Jessie shrugged her shoulders. "He's hit in the shoulder, and somewhere on the side of the head."

"He's losing blood fast." Even in the dark Ki could see the copious flow of blood.

"Help me get him up."

"Jessie, it might be dangerous to move him. There's a possibility that we might—"

"If we don't move him he'll surely bleed to death. Let's get him to my room."

"The back way," Ki suggested.

Jessie nodded her head. "The back way."

They managed to get the wounded man back to the hotel without much problem. The Kid let out a painful moan as they first lifted him, but then quickly dropped off into unconsciousness.

The instant they placed the outlaw on the bed, Jessie turned to Ki. "Get the doctor." She did not need to qualify it with a fast, hurry, or quick. She knew Ki would not waste a moment.

She snatched the enamel washbasin from her dresser and hurried out of the room. She returned a few seconds later with the bowl full of water. She would have liked to have seen if there was any hot water left in the kitchen, but she dared not waste any more time. She set to work cleaning up the bloody face of the Two Gun Kid.

Oddly enough, the more blood that filled the basin the better she felt. As Jessie washed away the blood, she saw more and more of the Kid's face. The wound, originally hard to find in the dark, seemed to be only a flesh wound above the Kid's right ear. She was about to roll him over to start cleaning his shoulder wound when the door creaked open.

Ki ushered in a tall, well-rounded gentleman, who looked like he would be more suited to wearing a lumber jacket and carrying an ax than to wearing a white shirt and wielding a scalpel. Jessie stepped back wordlessly, but her heart sank as she let the elderly doctor get a look at the patient. She had been hoping for a young doctor—someone who either would not recognize the Two Gun Kid or whose mind would not already be made up against the outlaw. Although the doctor's age did not necessarily mean he would disfavor the outlaw—after all, Wes liked the Kid—it stood to reason that the more respectable citizenry already had him pegged as a murderer.

But the doctor showed no sign of recognition. Jessie looked to Ki and wondered what he had told the doctor, but before Ki could say anything to her the doctor turned around. "We could use some fresh water. Hot if possible."

Ki nodded, took the washbasin, and left. Jessie moved to the other side of the bed. "How does he look, Doctor?"

"He's lost a lot of blood," he said noncommittally.

"But will he live?" she continued.

"We'll know more in a few minutes. Hold this lamp here if you want to be helpful."

Jessie took the hurricane lamp and held it over the Kid's body. The doctor propped the Two Gun Kid on his side and ripped his shirt clear off. He readied his tools in the hot water Ki brought back, then prepared the wound by sprinkling it with sulfur. After a few minutes of intense probing, his prongs removed the bullet from the hole. With a splash he dropped it into the basin. "It passed just south of his clavicle."

"The collarbone?" Jessie asked.

The doctor nodded. "The bone's not broken."

"And how about his head?"

"We'll get to that now. But it's not as serious as it looks." As the doctor promised, once the hair was shaved away there proved to be a long bloody crease running the length of the Kid's head. In spots, the raw white of his skull was exposed. But even Jessie could see that the wound was not a fatal one—at least not yet.

As he dressed the head wound, the doctor asked them, "How'd this happen?"

"Someone just rode up and put two into him from behind," Jessie stated simply.

The doctor gave her a reproachful look. "I didn't ask you to repeat the obvious."

"I can't tell you any more." That was almost true. "We couldn't see who it was; he was gone before we could have even gotten to our horses."

The doctor accepted that and nodded. "Your friend here is very lucky," he said, giving her a long hard stare. "An inch over on either shot, this one deeper into the head, and that one into the heart," he said, pointing, "and he would have been dead on the spot. When you get him home he'll have some stories to tell." The doctor stood up and looked squarely at Jessie.

Jessie looked at Ki, then at the doctor. "Doctor, I'd like to thank you for your help, but there's something you should know," she began hesitantly.

"My good lady, if you're about to tell me you have insufficient funds to pay for my services—"

"Oh, no. Of course not."

"Good, because I get my fee whether my patient lives or dies."

That brought a gasp from Jessie. "Will he . . . ?"

The doctor shrugged. "It's still too early to tell. He's lost a lot of blood, but barring infection I think he'll pull through."

Jessie sighed with relief. "But about this man . . ."

The doctor ignored her and set a roll of cloth and a tin of powder on the night table. "Change the bandages as needed, and sprinkle some more sulfur on the wounds. I'll be back in the morning. By then all the bleeding should have stopped."

"This man," she began again. This time her voice was firm, her mind made up. "There's something you should know about him, Doctor."

The doctor smiled as he stood up and rolled down his shirtsleeves. "There's little you could tell me about this man. I removed a rusty nail from his foot when he was no more than this high," he said and placed his hand just barely above his waist. "You might even still see the scar just below his right heel. It got pretty green and nasty." He picked up his bag and headed towards the door.

"But . . ." Jessie began.

"My fee, is it?" the doctor asked at the door. He shook his head slowly. "There is none."

Jessie, though confused, smiled. "One other thing, Doctor . . ."

The doctor nodded wisely. "I'll use the back way," he said, then was gone.

Jessie stepped closer to the bed and stared down at the outlaw. He had a strong, handsome face with a straight nose and flat forehead. Ki studied the expression on Jessie's face, a curious mixture of concern and relief. "I don't think there's anything more we can do for him, Jessie," he said sympathetically.

"It's such a miserable way to die, Ki. Shot in the back." Ki nodded but said nothing. Jessie raised her eyes to him. "I know what you're going to say." Jessie was well aware of his Oriental attitude toward death. To Ki, death was as natural as life. But Ki's answer surprised Jessie.

"There is no honor here," he said flatly. Coming from Ki, it was a remark of compassion and respect. In Ki's world, where death was not to be feared and could not be avoided, dying with honor was of supreme importance. "But I do not think he will die," he said with simple assurance.

"I guess we'll know more tomorrow."

"Jessie, I'm going to find this gunman. Why don't you sleep in my room?"

Jessie shook her head. "I'll sleep here in the chair. He may come to at any moment. Maybe he knows who might have shot him," she added hastily.

"Maybe," Ki answered.

"Though it's probably some glory-seeking coward looking to make a name for himself."

"If that were the case, why did the man flee? Wouldn't he be in the saloon right now boasting of his accomplishment?"

"Because we were there?" she wondered aloud. "We might be friends of the Kid's looking to avenge his shooting." It was a good theory, but she didn't totally believe it herself.

"Perhaps," Ki said as he headed to the door. "I don't

55

know how long this will take, but when I return we'll know more about this," he promised, then was gone.

Jessie sank into the upholstered chair. Though it was late and her body was tired, she did not sleep. It was probable she could not have even if she had wanted to; her mind was racing. From the onset, when she agreed to bring Marshal Dixon's murderer to justice, the solution to the problem seemed to be simply a matter of gathering the evidence and supplying solid proof. Surely the Two Gun Kid was guilty—at least most people thought so. But in the course of proving it, it turned out the outlaw had quite a few friends. Jessie was on the verge of reconsidering her original assumptions when again circumstances led her to believe that the Two Gun Kid was the one who had broken into their rooms. Why would anyone but a guilty party, with something to fear, search through their belongings? And then when the rider trailed them out to the Dixons, Jessie was again believing that the Two Gun Kid had killed the marshal.

But now, looking down at the gunman, she was more confused than ever. Not because he had friends; Jesse James had friends too, but that made him no less of a killer. And it was not the Two Gun Kid's engaging smile and polite manners that confused her; William Bonner was likewise noted for his courteousness, but that made him no less deadly. Not for a moment did the Kid's good manners lead Jessie to believe that he was incapable of the deeds attributed to him. On the contrary, his calm control convinced her that his reputation as a skilled gunfighter was probably very true. Jessie had faced many plug-uglies whose reputations far exceeded their skill. Bragging, boastful gunmen often did not have the goods to back up their positions as deadly gunfighters. Jessie could almost always spot these men. There was always something that gave them away. An overly exaggerated swagger, a nervous twitch, a shaky hand. There was always something to separate the deadly skilled from loud blowhards. But the

Two Gun Kid had been poised and polite. He made his intentions known; he ordered them to leave town. There was no threat in his voice, he was simply informing them of his intentions. If Jessie and Ki did not leave town, they would be gunned down. It was not an idle boast; it was a statement of fact. Only a man confident in his abilities as a gunfighter would do that.

And that put the biggest doubt in her mind. Why would a skilled gunfighter shoot his adversary in the back, sneaking up on him in a dark alley? The Two Gun Kid could have called the marshal out and shot him in a fair fight. A fight could always be instigated, the right insult could always be found, and the outlaw would be guilty of nothing more than shooting in self-defense. Even if Eugene had planned to walk away from a fight, the outlaw could have concocted a situation that could be construed as self-defense. In a tense moment between gunfighters it would always be questionable whether a man was just getting out of his chair or really going for his guns. No matter how Jessie looked at it, it made no sense for the outlaw to ambush the marshal in a dark alley. It not only lacked sense, it was downright stupid! And Jessie did not take the Two Gun Kid to be stupid.

And there was one other item that did not make sense. The Two Gun Kid clearly had the drop on Jessie and Ki. Was it likely that a killer who would shoot a marshal in the back would give two "lousy, stinkin' bounty hunters" a fair deal? If the outlaw suspected they were after him for a price, why didn't he shoot them dead on the spot? She had no answers, but plenty of questions.

Outside Ki did not concern himself with questions and answers; there were things that had to be taken care of first. He went right to the alley and found the spot where the Two Gun Kid was shot. Even in the dark he couldn't miss it; the dirt was stained with blood. Ki kicked dirt over the red stain and then meticulously retraced their steps. Every few feet he bent down and swished his hands on the ground as if he were trying to wash them in the dirt. What he was doing was covering their trail by wiping out the bloodstains that led right to the hotel's back door. He had no intentions of letting the outlaw, wounded or otherwise, endanger Jessie's life. It was likely that the assailant would come back to check on his handiwork, and if necessary finish the job. Ki did not want to leave a trail of blood leading right to Jessie's door. When he finished cleaning the hotel steps he went back out, feeling reasonably secure that Jessie was safe—at least for the time being. He found the thought amusing but he didn't have time to think on it any further. Soon there would be nothing but time, but now there were things to be done.

Back in the alley he searched for a suitable place of concealment. There was a pile of discarded barrels at the rear of the general store that would suffice if nothing better were to turn up. But given his druthers Ki preferred a high vantage point, not only for the better view but because most people tended to watch the ground more than they watched the sky. In his younger days Ki had wondered about the significance of that *ninja* observation. It had once seemed so full of symbolism and insight into the human condition. But now, older and wiser, Ki found the knowledge more utilitarian than philosophical. It was a means of getting him into places undiscovered, and of letting him remain there undetected. It had even saved his life a few times. Ki would never forget the time he had clung to the rafters of an old cabin while some wary plug-uglies checked everywhere. They looked under the beds and tables for him, when all they had to do was look above their heads. With that in mind, he decided on the roof of the general store. Though the flat roof was relatively open, the beams that helped support the large false front would be perfect. From there he could watch both the street and the alley.

Gaining access to the roof proved no problem, and Ki

was soon hunkered down at the front edge. He didn't know how long he would have to wait, but he was certain that eventually the Two Gun Kid's thwarted assassin would return to the alley. The assailant, not hearing anything about the death of the Two Gun Kid, would surely return to the scene of the crime for some clue as to the outlaw's whereabouts. With luck it would happen sooner than later. But either way, Ki knew he had time to kill.

Though he too had many questions and few answers, he did not trouble himself with them. Unless it was a spiritual exercise, as far as Ki was concerned, it was a waste of time to contemplate questions that one had no answer for. A mind could be enlightened in such a manner, but right now Ki was not looking for enlightenment. He was looking for a killer.

Instead of pondering unanswerable questions, he spent his energies combining little bits of information. Ki had also come to believe in the innocence of the Two Gun Kid. If he hadn't, he wouldn't have felt at ease leaving Jessie in the room alone with him. So that meant Marshal Dixon's killer was still unknown and on the loose, and so was the man who attempted to kill the Two Gun Kid. Ki had a hunch that the one might lead to the other.

Though Ki did not know who shot the outlaw, he had a pretty good idea of what the man was like. The way he conducted his business spoke much about his character. He was a coward at heart, who masqueraded as a loudmouthed braggart. He thought much of his modest abilities, but also had a fear of the Two Gun Kid. A less cocky man, less sure of his abilities, would have taken the extra time to unload all the contents of his six-shooter into the outlaw, not just two bullets. And a slightly braver individual would have done the same before fleeing on his horse. But the man was not without any shooting ability. Those were no chance shots that had dug into the Two Gun Kid's body. As the doctor had commented, one had been intended for the brain, the other for the heart. Either would have been instantly fatal; only the merest fraction of an inch kept the outlaw from a pine box. It might have been nothing more than chance that saved the Kid, but a competent assassin did not leave anything to chance.

In Ki's homeland of Japan, assassination was a fine art. *Ninjas,* men professionally trained in the art, would study for years to learn the tricks of the trade. Ki knew all there was to know about killing, and he knew a bungled assassination often revealed more than a successful one.

Prior to the attempt, the Two Gun Kid was almost unanimously suspected of killing the marshal. Most efforts would be concentrated on finding the proof that would bring him to the gallows. But even without proof, most of the debate would settle on the outlaw. Few would go looking elsewhere for the murderer. But now not only was the Two Gun Kid exonerated, at least in Ki's mind, but he had a very solid lead to the identity of the real murderer. All he had to do was wait.

Chapter 6

It was in the early hours of the morning that the Two Gun Kid started to toss and turn fitfully. Even though it was a cool night, the outlaw was bathed in a cold sweat. Jessie took a wet washcloth and began wiping his brow.

The Kid opened his eyes. "Annie . . ." he said with a smile.

"Lie still."

"Annie, you've come back . . ."

Jessie studied the man on the bed. His eyes, though clear and sharp, were not seeing straight. In his delirious state he thought Jessie to be another woman. "I've always been here," she told him, not wanting to excite him.

At that he smiled and closed his eyes. But a moment later they opened again. "Let's get back to the dance, Annie. I can hear those fiddles a playin'." He started to raise himself from the bed.

Jessie leaned closer and put a restraining hand on his shoulders. "Now, you just lie there," she said as she pushed him gently back against the pillows. It dawned on her then that she didn't know the outlaw's real name. Surely he wasn't always the Two Gun Kid. She was running different possibilities through her head, when she felt fingers running through her hair.

"You have the softest hair, Annie."

"Thank you." Jessie accepted the compliment with a smile, even though it was meant for another.

The Kid began to lift his head toward her, but groaned in pain at the effort. Jessie thought he was raising up to kiss her. Though she couldn't be certain, the thought gave her a rush of excitement. Impulsively she brushed her lips lightly against the Kid's. Jessie closed her eyes. It was a soft, almost innocent, kiss. She lifted her head and felt an odd mixture of excitement and embarrassment. Jessie had a sneaking suspicion she would have liked another kiss, and her desire embarrassed her even more. What would the outlaw think of her? She looked down at the Two Gun Kid; his eyes were closed, his breathing deep and peaceful. Jessie smiled. By morning he would remember nothing.

It seemed she was only in her chair a few moments when the Kid began to stir again. "Get me my boots. They'll be coming for me. . . ."

Jessie moved to his side. "No one's coming for you. You're safe here," she said soothingly, then realized he was still in the middle of a dream. It was only then that Jessie remembered the Kid still had his boots on. Before the doctor came she had been too busy cleaning up his wounds to worry about his boots. And after the doctor left she had sunk tiredly into the chair where she proceeded to worry over the Kid's chances of recovery, and then about the secondary issue of his guilt or innocence.

But it was time to make her patient more comfortable. She pulled off his boots, smiling to herself as she searched halfheartedly for the scar the doctor had mentioned. She didn't find it. The light was dim, and the Kid, once the cool air hit his sweaty feet, insisted on wiggling his toes contentedly. The irony there made her chuckle. It seemed incongruous that a feared killer would wiggle his toes as gleefully as any eight-year-old boy. Though there was no logic to it, that simple action further convinced Jessie that the Two Gun Kid was no murderer.

"Oh, Annie," the Kid sighed plaintively.

Jessie moved up and wiped his forehead again. "I'm here," she said softly.

The Two Gun Kid opened his eyes. "You have the sweetest smile I've ever seen."

"Lie quietly," she ordered sweetly.

"Kiss me again." Jessie blushed heavily. For a second she thought the Kid was fully conscious and aware of what she had done. "Lie down next to me," he continued. "I want to feel you close. I have to tell you . . ." He slipped back into his dreams without finishing the sentence.

Jessie felt his forehead. He was burning hot. After she had removed his boots she had thought of removing his pants as well, but had hesitated. Now she threw modesty aside. She felt it best to wipe his body down, then wrap him in the sheets. She undid his pants buttons, then pulled the trousers off over his ankles. With the cool rag she washed down his muscular legs.

"Oh, Annie, yes," the Kid moaned in his sleep.

As she washed down his legs she couldn't help but notice and admire his body. For the first time Jessie felt confident the Kid would live. He had lost a lot of blood, it was true, but there was still plenty left. She took the swollen, blood-engorged member that lay heavily between his legs as a sign of his improving health. Whoever she was, Annie was a lucky woman.

The rest of the night passed uneventfully. The doctor showed up in the morning, with a steaming pot of tea and a basketful of ham and biscuits.

"He's been sound asleep for the last few hours," Jessie informed the doctor. "Should I wake him to eat?"

"These aren't for him," the doctor explained with an amused smile, "they're for you."

Jessie had not thought of food at all, but with the smell

of the warm biscuits filling the room, she realized she was hungry. "I guess I could do with some food."

"You could do with some sleep, too." The doctor eyed her critically. "You won't do him any good exhausting yourself. Besides, he's healing fine."

"He was feverish last night."

"It's to be expected," the doctor explained. "His body is fighting off the infection."

"His wounds haven't become infected, have they?" Jessie asked with concern.

The doctor shook his head. "No, but with the loss of blood, any foreign substance could cause a problem." He straightened up and turned away from the patient. "Now, I meant what I said. I want you to rest up. I'll have to tend to you and there'll be a fee!" he warned sternly.

"I don't want to leave him. He might need something, or he might—"

The doctor cut her short. "My guess is he'll sleep well into the next day, then wake up hungry as hell. So you just get your sleep now, and don't fret too much about it."

Jessie nodded. She didn't have to be convinced further; she was tired. But after the doctor left, she went back into the chair, put her legs up on the edge of the bed, and made herself as comfortable as could be. She told herself she didn't want to take Ki's bed. He might come back any time and be in need of sleep himself. But she also knew she wanted to remain close to the Two Gun Kid.

The day passed with Jessie and the Two Gun Kid both sleeping soundly. In the evening a cool breeze blew into the room, and Jessie stretched awake. She was getting up and thinking about getting some dinner when she caught sight of the outlaw's guns on the night table. Out of curiosity she went over and picked them up.

They were beautifully crafted, silver-plated Colt Peacemakers. For Jessie's hands they were a little large, but even so, they were well balanced and had a nice feel to them. In the larger grip of the Two Gun Kid they probably felt like extensions of his own hands. The guns, handsome as they were, did not tell the whole story. Jessie had removed the Kid's double gunbelt when she took off his pants, but now she slipped one of the Colts into its holster. The holster was not decoratively tooled, and was not made of the soft leather many preferred for its comfort. The Two Gun Kid's holster was all business. It was made of a thick, hard leather that molded to the shape of the weapon. The gun, once holstered, would remain exactly where it was placed. Another interesting point in the construction of the holster was the way it held the revolver tilted forward. While that may have seemed awkward at first, it meant a man with a fast draw would have to raise his arm less to clear the gun barrel from the holster sheath. But the most telling detail about the holster, the item that proved its wearer worthy of his reputation, was its size and shape. The top portion of the leather holster was cut so that the gun butt, hammer, and trigger were all clearly exposed. The wearer of such a holster would give many a man reason to fear.

She was just sliding the revolver from its holster when she felt the cold eyes of the outlaw staring up at her. Something in his expression told her he was fully cognizant. Self-consciously Jessie put the handgun back down on the nightstand. "How are you feeling?"

The Two Gun Kid eyed her suspiciously. "I'd like some water."

Jessie poured him a glass of water. The Kid started to sit up, then winced in pain. "Here, let me help you," she said as she placed a hand behind his head. The Kid sipped at the water till the glass was drained, then sank back against the pillows. Jessie could see him studying the room. "Let me guess," she said with a smile. "You want to know where you are."

"I'm in your hotel room," he answered tiredly. "I just can't figure why."

"Very good." At first she was surprised that he knew

65

where he was, but then she realized it was not a hard deduction to come by. "How much do you remember?" she wondered aloud.

"Everything 'cept coming here."

"That's because you were out cold," Jessie explained. "We carried you here."

"Well, thank you for your hospitality, but I'll be on my way now."

Jessie did not bother to stop him; she didn't think he would get far. But he surprised her. He slowly pulled himself to a sitting position. "Where are my boots?" he asked as he swung his legs off the bed.

"I don't think you're in any shape to be going anywhere," Jessie said flatly.

The outlaw wasn't listening. Something had just struck him. "Hey, where are my pants?" he asked excitedly. He looked a bit nervous as he faced Jessie. Jessie's smile only seemed to fluster him more. "You didn't . . ."

"You're not the first man I've had to nurse," she stated patiently.

"I, ah, you didn't look at, ah, see, there was no call to . . ." He was blushing heavily as he stammered along.

"Why, if the feared Two Gun Kid isn't acting a mite modest!" Jessie said with a chuckle.

It was all too much for the Kid to stand. He lay back down in bed. "And you can lay off that 'Kid' stuff. I ain't a kid no more."

"Oh, I can see that for myself, Mr. Two Gun." Her voice was ripe with innuendo. "I got eyes . . ."

The outlaw turned beet-red, but proceeded undaunted. "I was a kid when they sentenced me to prison," he explained, "but a few years in the hole . . . an' you ain't a kid no more."

The solemn tone of his voice removed all playfulness from Jessie. She extended her hand. "I'm Jessica Starbuck," she said rather formally.

"Two Gun," her patient answered as he shook her hand.

Jessie would have liked it if he had used his real name. She was still curious about it. It even annoyed her that he didn't; after nursing him back to health she deserved to know his given name. A twinkle came back to her eye, and she smiled ever so sweetly. "But I reckon"—her eyes traveled swiftly over his body—"you can call me Jessie."

Again her innuendo found its mark, and the Kid blushed deeply. Jessie thought it ironic that a man capable of taking another man's life still found room for excessive modesty. It was almost perverse, the pleasure she was getting from this, but she reasoned it served the man right for sneaking up on her with drawn guns. She recalled the way he had held her and Ki at bay in the alley, and proceeded to taunt him some more. "Who is Annie?"

"Why?" Two Gun seemed confused.

"You were talking about her last night."

"Oh."

"You seemed to be having rather fond recollections."

Modesty or no modesty, Jessie had pushed Two Gun too far. "I didn't ask you to bring me here," he snapped.

"And I didn't ask to have you wave your guns in my face, and try to run me out of town," she shot right back at him.

"Well, I don't go round embarrassing a man, sticking my nose where it don't belong," he answered defensively.

"I don't make a habit of it. I was only trying to make you comfortable. But I reckon I should have left an old cuss like you to bleed to death in the alley!"

"I'm glad you didn't."

"I bet." Though he had sounded apologetic, Jessie was still fuming. Her cool green eyes were burning fire, her brow was knitted, and her lips were pursed. Two Gun couldn't help but notice.

"Mainly so's I'd get to make your acquaintance. You're lookin' awfully pretty now, Jessie."

"Well, you look a mess," she snapped, though she tempered her words with a smile.

"Reckon stopping slugs ain't one o' my strong points."

"I should hope not," Jessie said emphatically. "I wouldn't want you making a habit of this."

Two Gun let out a chuckle, but his face quickly screwed up in pain.

"Are you all right? Does it hurt much?"

Two Gun shook his head slowly. "Only when I laugh."

It was a long, hot day on the roof of the general store, and time moved slowly. In his haste, Ki had forgotten to take along adequate provisions. Though the lack of food did not present much of a problem, Ki found himself extremely thirsty.

By late afternoon he was about to give up his vigil and find some water when a man walked past the alley and stopped to lean against the wall of the store. Anxiously, Ki inched over the edge and waited for the man to betray his hand. But unfortunately, after rolling a smoke, the man went on his way.

Time after time this happened. Someone would approach, spark Ki's interest, then continue past without giving any attention to the alley.

Ki knew his physical discomfort was affecting his attitude. Parched and dry, he was looking for the quick solution, the easy way out. Any and every man was now viewed with suspicion. In his desire to find the gunman, he was ready to jump to quick conclusions. Still, he did not want to abandon his position. The few minutes he would be gone could be the moment chosen by the assailant to return to the scene of the crime. Then the day of waiting would be for nothing, and they would lose the one solid lead they had to finding the real murderer of Marshal Dixon. No, rather than risk that, Ki would endure a bit longer.

He kept a sharp eye on the street below, but turned his mind to more pleasing thoughts. Thoughts of wildflowers and soft, light-brown curls. Of blooming flowers and small, budding breasts with red-tipped nipples. Inside his mind he could feel the warmth of Katie's skin pressed tight against him, and the softness of the straw they had lain naked upon in the barn. The next time he went out to the house, he would take her on a long walk in the fields. They would watch the sun set, and make love. They would lie under the stars and let the cool night breeze caress their bodies. Ki would lavish kisses on Katie's firm breasts and run his tongue up the length of her satin-smooth thighs. Eventually his mind shifted from the future back to the past as he remembered their tryst in the barn. She had an eager, playful tongue herself. Ki smiled at his thoughts. The woman did have charm and considerable talent. Thinking of her talents brought her berry pie to mind. And with that Ki realized he had reached his limit.

It was the dinner hour, and the town was noticeably quieter, the streets less crowded. It would be some time before the saloon and the night activity came to life. It was a good time for Ki to take a break.

Ki was still a little hesitant to leave; there was always that slim chance he would miss something. But there was no denying he was hungry and in need of water. Climbing off the roof, he decided to go borrow a few items from the general store. Though it was closed, he would come back another time to pay for his purchases. Slipping through a back window, he entered the store quickly and silently.

Inside, Ki grabbed a tin of beans, a stick of jerky, and a canteen. On second thought he doubled his purchase, taking two of everything and throwing in a tin of tomatoes. He didn't like to think about it, but he might have to spend at least another day up on the roof. He might as well save himself a second trip now.

With more cans than he could easily handle, he went to the counter and grabbed a bandanna, which he folded into a makeshift sack. The bandanna would free his hands for the climb back to the roof and also come in handy as a cooling washrag. There was one other thing he needed—a large knife or suitable can opener. He could use one of his *shurikens,* but he didn't like to dull the sharp points of his throwing stars. There was probably an opener bolted to the edge of the counter. Stepping behind the counter he did indeed find what he was looking for, but he also found something else that sparked his curiosity.

As he finished opening the tin of beans, he noticed there was a safe nestled under the counter. Though Ki found it odd that a store this size would have need for such a solid safe, there were always a few proprietors who would rather lock their money away on their own premises than give it over to the bank. And the way some banks were run Ki could not blame them. Just because a bank was in the business of safeguarding one's money, that did not always mean they did their job well. Like any business, there were those companies that ran efficient operations and those that did not. It was no coincidence that some banks were robbed time and again while others retained their reputations for having never been robbed.

Therefore, having a small vault under the counter did not necessarily raise any undue suspicions. But Ki had seen the proprietor leave the store and go over to the bank. And that *did* raise a few questions. Ki was certain the store owner had been carrying money over to the bank; he had a cautious look on his way to the bank, and a more casual gait on his return. If he was depositing his money in the bank, what was in the safe under the counter? More often than not, Ki had found that people with safes had things to hide. But it was another mystery that would have to wait to be solved. Right now Ki wanted to fill his canteen with water and get back to his rooftop perch.

Chapter 7

The door creaked open. The two Gun Kid, alerted by the turn of the handle, had his Peacemaker trained on the door. Whoever was sneaking into the room was in for a surprise.

Jessie backed into the room, then turned to find the outlaw's shiny gun once again pointed right at her. "I wish you'd stop pointing that thing at me," she said as she placed a tray of food on the dresser.

"I didn't know it was you," he said as he laid the gun back down on the table.

"I'm sorry. I should have told you I was going for some food, but I didn't want to wake you."

"Maybe I'm just a little too cautious myself," the outlaw said by way of an apology.

"Who *were* you expecting?" As she said it, Jessie realized it was a darn good question. A shrug was the only response she got. Nonetheless, she pursued the issue. "Then why the warm greeting?"

"Whoever shot me last night might be coming back to finish the job."

"And you have no idea who that might be?"

The outlaw shook his head. "It's not that I don't have any enemies, Jessie. It's just that I don't have any who would be holding a grudge that long."

"I don't follow."

The Kid smiled. "I've only been out a few weeks. Barely enough time to make more'n a dozen enemies. . . ." Jessie did not seem amused. "It's a joke," he added as he saw the serious look that remained on her face.

"Is it?" she questioned aloud. "Someone out there isn't too fond of you, Two Gun."

"But I don't have an inkling as to who it might be. Like I said, when you're cooling your saddle behind bars, most folks forget the grievances they had against you. You come out and, if you're not totally forgotten, then at least most of the hate is."

"I'm sorry I brought it up, Two Gun."

"Don't be, Jessie. I tell you, it ain't any harder to talk about it than it was to live through. If you feel there's somethin' you want to know. . ."

"All right."

"I mean it." It seemed important for the outlaw to make his point clear. "It's not that I like talkin' 'bout it, Jessie. But I don't want to make you feel uncomfortable, or nothin'. Anything you want to know, ask."

"Maybe I will, but for now let's eat while it's hot. Do you like chicken and dumplings?"

"My all-time favorite," he responded eagerly.

"I'm glad to see you have an appetite," Jessie remarked as she watched the Kid clean his plate.

"Good food is a simple pleasure."

Jessie wondered what role prison had played in that philosophical thought, but she didn't ask. Surprisingly, Two Gun seemed to have read her thoughts. "Don't worry, Jessie," he said with a smile. "I had a hardy appetite even before I did my time. Some things even prison life can't kill. But never mind all that, there's something I'd like to say."

"Well, go ahead," Jessie urged, after Two Gun paused an unusually long time.

"I'm not always too good at setting things straight. But I reckon you're not who I thought you were."

"Why do you say that?"

"'Cause if you were, you would have just let me die in the alley. The money comes either way. Least that's what most posters say—'Dead or Alive.'"

"Well, I'm glad we got that cleared up. But I don't understand why you thought Ki and I were after you in the first place. Is there still a bounty on your head?"

"Not any longer."

"Then there shouldn't be anyone interested in you."

"You'd think not," the outlaw replied. "But there's always one or two who are a little slow in hearing. Either they've been out on a trail so long they ain't heard the news, or—"

"They'd have to have been gone an awful long time!" Jessie interjected.

"Or they're just looking for another notch in their belt."

"But that's murder."

Two Gun shrugged. "They have an old wanted poster in their vest pocket—how do they know you're not wanted anymore?"

"But they don't get their money."

"Depends. If it's the government, no. But if it's a freight company, or the railroads, sometimes they'll pay. They think it acts as a deterrent."

"But still . . ."

Two Gun ignored her protest. "Even if there's no money, it's a feather in their cap. Makes their services more appealin' for their next job. The bounty hunter who brings in the Two Gun Kid, wanted or not, is gonna get a lot of respect."

"Even if he shoots you in the back in a dark alley?"

"Even so. People don't remember the triflin' details," he said with a chuckle.

"You don't seem too troubled by the idea," Jessie said with a surprising amount of annoyance. She was finding herself liking Two Gun, and didn't want to see him killed because of his carelessness.

"There isn't much I can do about it," he said with a warm smile. "'Cept keep my guns loaded and nearby."

Jessie thought there was much more he could do, but she didn't think this was the time to be preaching reform. Instead she apologized. "And you're not who I thought you were."

"Now, why do you say that?"

"Because you're not the killer I thought you were."

"You mean, Marshal Dixon?"

Jessie nodded. "You didn't." It wasn't a question, but Two Gun shook his head nonetheless. "But if you didn't, who did?"

"I'd like to know that myself." There was an iron coldness to his words. Jessie could see his jaw set firmly.

With his hunger and thirst both satiated, Ki began to reconsider the situation with a clear head. Though his logic and reasoning were sound, that was no guarantee the Two Gun Kid's assailant would return to the alley. The man's cowardly nature could far outweigh his curiosity. For all Ki knew, right now the man could be enjoying a cool beer in another county. But Ki doubted that. No one had had even the slightest look at the assassin; a few fleeting seconds on a dark night do not reveal many details. The killer could walk up to Ki and ask for a match and Ki would be no wiser. And the man knew that. An unidentifiable man need not fear exposure; anonymity made shy men bold.

Ki did not need to have total faith in his plan. He just needed to follow it until the killer returned, or a new and better course of action revealed itself. Ki hunkered down, knowing that in due course, one or the other would prevail. He did not have a strong preference; whatever path led to Marshal Dixon's murderer would be fine. But he experienced a sudden rush when he saw Tucker slowly saunter down the street.

He strolled along the far boardwalk looking very much at ease, but when he came opposite the alley he came to a stop. Leaning up against one of the posts he bit off a hunk of chewing tobacco. Tucker's eyes squinted almost closed as his jaw worked away at the wad in his mouth. Ki could almost hear the plug-ugly's brain working. He smiled to himself as he imagined the man's thoughts: *Where in hell is that damned body?*

Tucker stepped out into the street and took one step toward the alley. Ki sat up on the balls of his feet ready to spring down, but then the man changed his mind and turned away. Ki wondered if Tucker was too stupid to check the alley for clues, or too wary of being noticed by any possible watchers.

Ki was determined to find out. He watched Tucker enter the Silver Lode Saloon, then nimbly climbed off the roof and walked hurriedly to the saloon. One way or the other he would get some answers.

"I reckon it's time you heard the truth, Jessie," Two Gun said with a heavy sigh.

"Then you do know something about who murdered Eugene," Jessie said excitedly.

"Not really," the Kid said slowly. "But I know that they weren't intending to kill him."

Jessie's heart sank. She couldn't be sure what Two Gun meant. Was he trying to tell her that he did in fact shoot the marshal, but it was an accident? Jessie looked him squarely in the eyes. She was positive that wasn't the case. She thought it over, then chose her words very deliberately. "Two Gun, if you're harboring a killer because you think it was an accident, or if you know something you're keeping a secret, you might be responsible for letting the killer escape."

"Jessie, I'm responsible for his death!"

Jessie's jaw dropped; her body stiffened. Her world seemed to fall away as crazy thoughts raced through her head. How could it be! How could the man she had nursed back to health be the murderer of her good friend? The man she had watched over, fed and even kissed, had put two bullets into her friend's back to end his life in a dirty alley. She sat there not knowing what to do. Two Gun continued talking and she slowly shifted focus to hear his words.

". . . it's not as if I pulled the trigger . . ."

Jessie closed her eyes and shook her head, trying to clear the confusion. "I'm sorry, Two Gun, I don't understand."

The outlaw was patient. "I was saying that even though I didn't shoot him, I'm responsible for the marshal's death. It's my fault he's dead, Jessie."

"I hear what you're saying, but I don't understand it," she said simply.

"How could you?" He stared at her, seemingly wanting something that was beyond her ability to give. "I better start at the beginning." The Kid lowered his head to the pillow and stared up at the ceiling.

"I trust you, Two Gun. I'll believe what you have to say."

The outlaw turned to her and nodded his head. "My papa always said, 'No matter how big a barn you're buildin' you always start with the first board.' I reckon that holds true for storytelling, too."

"There's no hurry," Jessie assured him. "Tell it to me any way you want."

"It ain't so complicated, 'cept for the parts I don't have an answer to . . ."

"Maybe together we can figure things out."

76

The outlaw smiled. "It goes back to when Marshal Dixon caught up with me at Willow Springs. It took me a heap of figurin', too. See, good as he was, Dixon never would have found me if it wasn't that I was betrayed."

"By whom?" Jessie jumped to the question.

"I spent a good many months wonderin' 'bout that myself. I always thought it was this yahoo Jeffrys I once rode with. Everything seemed to fit, till they hung him up in Topeka for the shooting of a railway clerk. He had an alibi so good they stretched his neck for it. He couldn't have been talking to the posse that was after me and also be in Topeka."

"Then you never found out who betrayed you?"

The outlaw nodded. "That's why I came here."

"Most people think you came here looking for Marshal Dixon."

"I did, but not for the reasons they thought."

"You didn't come here gunning for the marshal." It was not really a question.

"I came here to talk with him. I could run things over in my head night after night and still not get anywhere. I needed to find the squealer."

"And you thought the marshal would tell you. But he didn't?"

"He never got the chance to."

Jessie was confused. "But people said you were in town for a few days before he was shot."

The outlaw nodded. "I didn't think it sensible to go ridin' up to Dixon's door."

"I can see why," Jessie agreed readily. "Even Eugene might misinterpret that kind of behavior."

"No," Two Gun said as he shook his head. "The marshal knew he had nothing to fear from me."

"Then why—" Jessie began.

"I had a lot of respect for him, Jessie. Hell, I was much beholden to that man."

77

"That's an odd thing to say about the man who sent you off to prison." Jessie's expression matched the surprised tone of her voice.

"That's exactly why I was grateful. Marshal Dixon got to me a scant few hours before the posse of bounty hunters and vigilantes. If it wasn't for Marshal Dixon they would have stretched my neck on the spot."

Jessie was beginning to get the picture. "The posters do say 'Dead or Alive,'" she said in a poor attempt at humor.

"An' there's some folks who have a real hankerin' for a necktie party. The marshal not only kept them at bay, but he made sure I got a fair trial."

"He was an honest man," Jessie said fondly.

Two Gun agreed. "He was one of the few who saw me for what I was, an' not for all the stories that were told 'bout me. I never killed a man who wasn't shooting at me first. An' I never killed that clerk in the First City Bank. And at the trial there were witnesses who said so."

"Friends you didn't know you had?" Jessie wondered out loud.

The outlaw nodded. "But Marshal Dixon believed me right from the start."

"He was a good judge of character."

"But he was also more. He seemed to have a real concern for me, like he had taken a liking to me."

"I can understand that, Two Gun. I think maybe he saw a little bit of himself in you."

The outlaw nodded enthusiastically. "On the way back he talked to me like I was kin. Like he could straighten me out, and like he wanted to help me."

"That was Eugene." Jessie's voice was thick, and the memory of her friend clouded her vision with tears.

The Two Gun Kid was also affected by his recollections of the marshal. His voice held a pleading tone. "When it was time to go, it was like saying good-bye to a friend. I like to think the marshal felt the same."

"I'm sure he did, Two Gun."

The outlaw nodded but said nothing. A few moments

78

passed in silence, then with a loud sigh Two Gun continued his tale. "Like I said, I had a lot of respect for the marshal. I didn't know how it would look for him to be seen with me, what it would mean to his reputation. . . ."

"He wouldn't turn you away, regardless of—"

"I know that, Jessie." Two Gun cut her off sharply. "But I was thinking of what the others might make of it. What the townspeople would say behind his back."

"He wouldn't pay them any mind," Jessie repeated strongly.

Two Gun shrugged. "There are a lot of people who think I got a fortune stashed away in the hills."

"Do you?"

"Not a fortune," he said with a boyish smile. "But those people who didn't think I came gunning for him would think I came to pay him off for the fair treatment he'd shown me."

"He was only doing his duty," Jessie said logically.

"We know that," the outlaw said dryly, "but others'd think I owed him a debt for being square with me—and I do. So I reckoned I'd wait for him to come to town, and then real casually arrange a chance to talk with him alone."

"But that chance never came," Jessie remarked almost to herself. She could see the events unfolding, though she still couldn't understand what they meant.

"Not exactly," Two Gun continued. "Finally, the marshal rode into town. While he was having a drink in the saloon, I wandered in and caught his eye. I made sure he saw me slip out to the alley."

"You figured you could get a few minutes alone with him out back?"

"I thought no one would be the wiser."

"But you were wrong." Jessie avoided saying it, but to herself she phrased it as "dead wrong."

"Yes and no. Someone had seen me go into the alley, but they didn't see the marshal."

"How do you know that?" Jessie demanded.

"It was a dark night, Jessie. I was standing against the

wall. You wouldn't have spotted me till you tripped over me. But someone knew I was out there."

"Besides Eugene?"

"I was just stepping away from the wall to talk to the marshal when someone fired two shots." He swallowed hard. "He was dead before he hit the ground."

"It still makes no sense. Who would want to kill Eugene?"

"Don't you see, Jessie?" Two Gun cried out. "No one wanted to shoot the marshal. They wanted me! Jessie, no one knew the marshal was out there!"

The pieces were just beginning to fit in place. "So whoever wanted you dead killed the marshal by mistake. If we can find that person we have the killer."

"Right. I reckon he saw me leave the Silver Lode and step into the alley."

"And he never knew the Marshal was there because he left the saloon ahead of him," Jessie added excitedly.

"That's the way I see it, too."

"Why didn't you tell anyone this?" Jessie said with all sincerity. The look the Two Gun Kid gave her needed no words. "I guess you're right, no one would believe you."

"Not only that, but everyone in the saloon heard two shots."

"So?"

"They were fired at almost the same time."

"That means from two guns. . . ." As soon as she said it, Jessie understood.

"Around these parts that's a sort of trademark of mine." There was no pride in his voice, but there was no shame either.

There was nothing further to say. Jessie sat there and mentally rearranged all the information, looking for something that could give them a clue. But unfortunately she was coming up blank.

The Two Gun Kid, though, was still wrapped up in the tragic events of that night. "Those two bullets were meant for me. Because of me, Marshal Dixon is dead."

Jessie got up and went over to his side. "You can't blame yourself," she said as she reached out for his cheek.

The Two Gun Kid wasn't listening. "So you see, I have a double score to settle," he said. "First for the attempt on my life, and more importantly, for the murder of a friend."

Chapter 8

Ki threw back the batwings and strode into the saloon. He hardly took notice of Cooper working behind the bar. Another time, there were things he wanted to discuss with the bartender, but now Ki made straight for the corner gaming table, where Tucker already had a place.

"There space for another hand?" Ki asked as he pulled back an empty chair.

The well-dressed gentleman who was seated to Tucker's right looked up. "This here's a friendly game, mister. You want to test your skill, the house tables are over there."

"A friendly game of chance is fine with me," Ki persisted.

"Well, friend," the well-dressed man said as he twirled his waxed mustache, "I'll take your money same as the next."

"You're more than welcome to try," said Ki as he sat down. Tucker shifted uneasily in his seat. "What's the game?"

"Straight draw. Two bits and a buck."

"What's the house cut?" Ki asked as he dug into his pants and pulled out a small roll of bills.

The short man to the left of Ki let out a chuckle. "Reckon he is new to these parts, Luke."

The well-dressed man nodded. "My name's Hollowell, Luke Hollowell." Ki noted that the man did not offer his hand. "I *am* the house, friend," he continued. "I own this here saloon. An' like I said, this here's a congenial game, a leisurely repose between me an' my friends."

"Glad to be sitting in," Ki said with a smile. He studied the three men who shared the table with him. Tucker he was already familiar with; only the man's unease was worth noting. The man on his other side was a round-faced gent, who Ki surmised from his dress was one of the town's merchants. With his soft, fleshy hands and red, bulbous nose Ki expected little trouble from him. He was probably nothing more than a bar buffalo who spent his nights in the saloon drinking, watching the dance girls, and playing cards. Ki would get no information from that one.

Ki now studied the man opposite him. Hollowell was in his early thirties. He was tall, with dark hair and matching mustache. His hair was slicked back and shining brightly. And as he had been the other night, he was impeccably dressed in a dark vested suit. The faint aroma of witch hazel enveloped the man. A question immediately came to Ki's mind: What was a man like Luke Hollowell doing with the likes of Tucker? There was only one answer. Tucker was the man's lackey. When there was something that needed doing, when Hollowell didn't want to soil his hands, he would send Tucker. Had Hollowell sent Tucker to murder the Two Gun Kid? Their association did not in itself implicate the saloon owner in murder; but he would bear close watching.

Hollowell raised his hand, and a shapely saloon girl, her legs wrapped in black net stockings and her bosom pressing out from her red satin dress, scurried over. "Maude, get our friend a drink, on the house, and a stack of coins."

83

She took a few bills from Ki and returned shortly with a shotglass and a shiny pile of quarters. Hollowell dealt the first hand.

The game proceeded without much excitement. Ki won a few hands, lost a few. But that was immaterial. Ki's only interest was in studying Tucker, Hollowell, and the relationship between the two. Tucker said little, while Hollowell kept up an easy and uninformative chatter. After so many hands, the third man, the one Ki took for a town merchant, stood up and announced pleasantly, "I think it's time for me to stretch a bit and get some fresh air."

"All right, Ed, see you tomorrow," Hollowell said pleasantly. Ki wondered if there had been a sign between the two that he had missed. After forty minutes of play, it was no accident Ki had almost the exact same amount of money as when he entered the game. The challenge of cards held little interest for Ki. Life itself was enough excitement; every day was another challenge. Ki found honest poker required a certain amount of luck; there was always the unpredictability of the cards. But that was honest poker. Ki had sat in many a saloon and could count on his fingers the number of totally honest card games he had watched. They had varied in intensity of dishonesty from completely rigged games with marked decks, to games where two players worked in silent partnership to manipulate the odds in their favor. Sometimes the only skill involved in these games of chance was in detecting the manner in which one was to be separated from one's money.

Ki was not an especially good poker player, but he was a very astute observer of human nature. He could almost sense what would come next. The only wonder was whether Tucker or Hollowell would initiate it.

It was Tucker. The plug-ugly counted his money and scratched at his whiskers, seemingly deep in thought.

"Maybe Ed's right. This game'll go on all night," he said in a disgruntled voice. "'Tain't no fun three-handed, least thisaway."

"What are you suggesting, Tucker?" Hollowell asked in as innocent a voice as he could muster.

"Let's raise the stakes. Make it a sight more interestin'. One big loser or one big winner!"

"I don't know. What do you say, friend?" Hollowell asked as he shuffled the cards smoothly.

Ki looked thoughtful. "I seem to be holding my own. Why not?"

"Then how 'bout we say two bucks and twenty."

"Fine with me," Ki said with a nod.

Hollowell swiveled in his chair and turned to the bar. "Cooper, let's have another round of drinks here." As he turned around the deck of cards remained in his hand, though briefly his twisted body shielded his hand from Ki's sight. When he turned back to the table Ki had no doubt that the deck of cards Hollowell held in his hand was not the same deck they had been using earlier.

Hollowell was now all business. He kept up the same idle talk, but there was a stiffness to his posture that wasn't there before. It was very subtle, but Ki also thought he dealt the cards a little more crisply than before.

Ki assumed he would have a few hands' grace before they moved in for the kill. That they were working in tandem there was no doubt; with constant regularity, when Hollowell dealt, Tucker won.

Ki was a little troubled. That they were cheating and that he could lose his money didn't bother him in the least. But Ki had not joined the game to be fleeced. He had come looking for information, and he wanted to leave knowing more than that Hollowell was a cheat and Tucker was his lackey. He would gladly lose all the money on the table to learn what Tucker's motives were for shooting the Two

85

Gun Kid. Ki was not paying attention to the cards. He was smugly thinking if money couldn't get the information he wanted he could always try to beat it out of the man. He justified his rash thought by asking himself how many honest people had been swindled out of their hard-earned money by these two lowlifes.

As Ki threw in his ante, an odd thought struck him. But he had to be sure. He picked up his cards as they were dealt, but looked Hollowell straight in the eye. "From what happened here the other night I thought the bartender owned the saloon."

"He has an interest in it. We're partners," the gambler answered freely.

"Well, any way you slice it, it's a nice pie to have your hand in," Ki said a bit naively. "A man who owns a saloon like this musn't have too many financial worries." He turned directly to Tucker. "Why, if I had a place like this I'd be set for life," he added with a touch of awe. Tucker played right into his hands.

"Mr. Hollowell owns quite a bit more in these parts than just the Silver Lode."

"That so?" Ki said with genuine interest.

"We can discuss my business ventures at length, Mr. . . . ?"

"Ki."

"Yes, some other time perhaps, but right now the bet is to you." Hollowell neatly fanned his cards and waited impatiently for Ki.

Without pause for thought Ki threw in a silver dollar. The game suddenly took on higher stakes than money; Ki's suspicions were verified. To the man who owned the saloon and, in his own words, other business ventures, all the money on the table was nothing more than pocket change. Ki was being set up all right, but not for his money. Were they on to him? Did these two men know what he was up to?

When the bet came back to him he studied his cards

momentarily. He was not thinking about his hand, he was thinking about the situation—perhaps deadly situation— he was in. The facts raced through his mind. For the same reason he could not identify Two Gun's assailant, the assailant had no way of identifying him. But Tucker had been antagonistic to him from the start. There was no mistaking that. The night he brought in Greene's body, Tucker had been taking his cue from Hollowell. Why?

On the draw, Ki decided to throw in his cards. "Reckon the cards aren't going my way," he said to no one in particular. He needed a few moments undisturbed to think this through.

Ki studied the two men as they played out the hand. Though it was irrelevant who won, they put on a good show. To eliminate whatever suspicions an observer might have, each bet, each raise was well acted. The hand even went on a bit longer than was necessary. Both men wanted to assure Ki there was no teamwork going on here. Ki appreciated their act; it gave him the time to formulate his course of action.

Ki should have seen it sooner, but it was better late than never. Tucker's posture was always defensive—too defensive for an honest man. Even out in the street, when Tucker wanted to step into the alley to have a closer look, he hesitated. Surely he could not have known Ki was there waiting for him, but yet he hesitated. Ki already knew the man to be cowardly at heart. And cowards, especially murderous ones, tended to be excruciatingly careful. Tucker didn't know what business Ki had here in Coleville, but he did know that the half-Oriental stuck his face in at all the awkward moments. The marshal was killed, Greene was found murdered, and Ki showed up asking questions about the Two Gun Kid. Ki smiled to himself. Sometimes being in the right place at the right time accounted for much.

Cooper suspected Ki of being up to something. The Kid suspected Ki of being a bounty hunter. Why shouldn't Tucker and Hollowell have their suspicions? If Tucker was guilty of something, he'd just as soon dispose of an inquiring, nosy stranger than run the risk of being discovered. Ki looked across the table at Tucker. Men like him thought nothing of killing first and asking questions later. And if they could goad him into a fight, or a situation that could be construed as self-defense, all the better.

Ki couldn't think of a better ruse than a high-stakes poker game. Tensions would be running high; at the merest indication of cheating lead would fly. No one would hold someone responsible for shooting a cheater, especially if the cardsharp made the first move.

Ki eased back in his chair; rather than being nervous, he was calm and relaxed. There was one way to beat them at their game, and Ki was going to enjoy doing it.

It was his deal. He shuffled the cards smoothly, for the first time exhibiting a little more dash than he had before.

Although Ki cared little for card games, he knew quite a bit about card manipulation. The long voyage from Japan had been spent with a master of the art. (Ki suspected the third mate had plied his former craft once too often, and had serendipitously embarked on a lengthy sea cruise— and a change of career. All the same, he had taught Ki well.) Ki had not been that interested in learning the finer skills of poker, but he had been fascinated by the sleight of hand, and the dexterity involved in slick dealing. Adept at the martial arts, Ki already had the physical strength and tactile sensitivity required to produce the small, quick hand movements. And Ki was about to exercise those muscles.

He continued to shuffle the deck, getting the feel of the cards. From simple observation alone, he had guessed the aces to be shaved. In other words, they were not perfectly rectangular. They were cut narrower at one end and wider at the other. It allowed for a skilled dealer to pull an ace out at any time. It also explained the numerous hands Tucker won with aces up. Ki's sensitive fingers also picked up slight pinpricks in many of the other cards; but that did not really concern him. The aces would do the trick.

"Think it'll be a scorcher tomorrow?" Ki asked blandly as he dealt the cards. He didn't need to cover his sleight of hand with distracting conversation, but he had been taught to do so, and he did it as naturally as he skimmed off the bottom of the deck. "It was plenty hot for me today. How 'bout you, Tucker?"

"Deal them cards," the man snapped irritably.

Ki smiled to himself. The man's irritation would rise when he looked at the cards. He turned affably to Hollowell. "The heat tends to make people a bit short. . . ." He got no response from the man.

Tucker picked up his cards. Ki studied the man, but he either had the perfect poker face, or he was too stupid to realize he was being set up. By this time Ki decided it was the latter. Tucker's scarred knuckles confirmed he did more thinking with his fists than with his head.

Ki played a conservative hand, seeing the bets, but only that. On the raise before the draw Hollowell folded. Good, that would make it simpler. Ki was pleasantly surprised to find on the draw Tucker threw in only one card. Ki knew he had two pairs. It was no great feat of deduction. He could not be pulling for a straight or a flush. Ki knew he held one pair; he had dealt him the two aces. The other pair had happened by sheer chance. Ki smiled to himself; even in a crooked deal lady luck played a part.

Ki looked down at his cards—a six, seven, jack, and pair of tens—and quickly changed his mind. Initially he didn't care who won the hand, just so long as Tucker and Hollowell knew two could play the game. But with Tucker holding two pairs Ki might as well have some fun—and win some money. Again, the money in itself didn't matter, but what did matter was the irritation it would cause Tucker. No one liked to lose a hand, especially when he was dealt two pairs.

Ki broke up his pair and threw in one of the tens. That left him with four cards—unrelated save for the fact they were all red, all diamonds. Any experienced player would

89

have done the same. Against an opponent holding twin pairs, one's only chance was to gamble on the flush. Professional players would have been able to tell the odds of pulling the flush, but even a novice knew the odds were not good. Experienced gamblers would have played a hunch. A simple cowhand would close his eyes and pray for the best. Ki did neither. He was by no means the most skillful poker player, but he was a very skilled dealer. For Ki there was no gamble.

He gave Tucker his card, then took his own card, very slyly, off the bottom.

Tucker glanced briefly at his one card, then trained his eyes on Ki. He was no doubt trying to read the signs. Ki acted casual, but an observer might construe his manner as a valiant effort at hiding disappointment. Of course, a shrewd observer might sense a trick, but no one would ever mistake the brooding Tucker for being shrewd.

"I bet twenty," Tucker said proudly as he placed a crumpled bill into the center of the table.

Wordlessly, Ki met the bet and raised him another twenty. At that Tucker seemed annoyed. "You don't expect me to turn tail on this one, do you, friend?" Ki said with exaggerated emphasis on the last word.

"You're free to throw away your money," Tucker growled back, "but it'll cost you another twenty."

Ki added his money to the pot. "I don't scare easily, Tucker." There was a veiled threat to his words that went beyond the confines of the poker table. "How about you? Willing to risk another twenty?"

"I'm calling your bluff, Chinee!" Tucker spat out thickly.

Ki remained calm. "You paid enough for the privilege."

Tucker slammed down his hand and spread out his cards. "Aces and eights!"

Ki smiled broadly. "The dead man's hand!" This was a twist of fate too good to pass up. "I'd be careful where I sat with a hand like that," he added ominously.

90

Tucker went livid at the reference to the hand Wild Bill Hickok held when he was shot in the back while playing cards in Deadwood. "Shut up!" he snapped. Tucker's fingers were itchy for the pot; they hovered around the pile ready and eager to herd it in. "Let's see yer hand."

"Happy to oblige," Ki said as he laid his cards down one by one. "Six . . . seven . . . ten . . . jack . . ." Ki held up his last card. "Care to make one more side wager?" He turned briefly to Hollowell, but kept a careful eye on Tucker. There were no takers. "Then kindly take your hands off my money."

When Ki had shuffled the deck he had palmed a card, noticed what it was, then sent it to the bottom. It was the first rule of dealing; know your bottom card. Sometimes it made no difference, but then at others . . .

Ki threw down his last card, the queen of diamonds.

"Damn! A flush." It did not need saying, but Tucker was beyond controlling himself. He was clearly at the point of exploding when Hollowell calmed him.

"Easy, Tucker. There are other hands to play." There was no mistaking Hollowell's meaning, and Tucker eased back into his chair greedily awaiting his cards and his revenge.

Hollowell raked in the cards and shuffled the deck. He acted as if nothing out of the ordinary had occurred. He slid the deck to Ki.

Ki hesitated, deciding whether to cut the cards or let them stand. Slowly he placed his hand on the deck, his fingers feeling for the exposed edges. "How long have you known Tucker?" he asked Hollowell.

"It's been a good many years."

"I hope he hasn't been cheating you for all of them," Ki announced flatly. With a quick hand movement he flipped out all four aces and threw them on the table. He kept a careful eye first on Tucker, and then on Hollowell.

At first Tucker seemed immobilized, frozen with shock. But then the blood rushed to his face. "He switched decks on us," Ki continued, knowing it was only a matter of seconds before Tucker struck.

Tucker's body started to rise from the chair. "You lying skunk!"

Suddenly, Ki flipped the table over onto Hollowell. That exposed a clear avenue to Tucker. The man's gun was coming out of his holster. Ki dove into him headfirst.

On impact the sixgun went off, and as the two tumbled to the floor, the gun slipped from Tucker's grasp. Ki rolled nimbly to his feet, but Tucker, the wind knocked from him, rested on his knees. Out the corner of his eye Tucker saw his sixgun lying just a few feet away. He made a quick, desperate lunge for it.

Ki saw it coming. First he brought his right foot down squarely in the middle of Tucker's back. Tucker fell face-down into the floorboards, his jaw hitting with a loud crunch. Stepping on top of the man, his left foot kicked the gun under a far table. He turned to see what Hollowell was up to, but he was just pushing the table off his lap.

A loud shotgun blast rocked the walls of the saloon. The crowd all turned to the bar, where Cooper had his scatter-gun pointed right at Ki. "Let him up," he ordered quietly. Ki removed his foot, and Tucker, his lip bleeding, stood up.

"There'll be no fighting in my saloon," the bartender continued.

"He called me a cheat," Tucker bellowed. Ki was glad the man's jaw was not broken. Tucker still had some talking to do.

"That so?" Cooper asked.

"He said I switched decks," Tucker said, advancing toward Ki.

"Hold it, Tucker," the bartender warned.

Tucker stopped in his tracks, but continued his verbal assault. "I think the Chinee switched them," he said, pointing an accusing finger. "He's the cheat!"

The bartender looked from one to the other. "There's

one way to tell. Empty yer pockets, both of you."

"There's no need for that." Hollowell had extricated himself from the overturned table and was approaching the two men. "There's been no real harm done." He stepped up to Ki and handed him a wad of money. "Take it and get the hell out."

Ki understood immediately why Hollowell did not want him or Tucker to empty their pockets. If neither of them had changed decks, that left only Hollowell, and it was important that his reputation remain untarnished. The hell with what people thought about Tucker. Ki took the money, but was wondering what his next move should be when Tucker made the decision for him.

"The hell you say." Tucker spat blood on the floor. "That stinkin' Chinee called me a cheat. No one does that!"

Cooper shifted nervously. "I don't give a whit what someone calls you, Tucker—"

"I'm gonna make him eat his words," Tucker promised, as he wiped more blood from his mouth. "I'm gonna make him sorry his stinkin' mama ever—"

"Settle your differences some other time," Cooper said calmly. Ki realized the bartender was trying to help him out of a sticky situation.

"He called me a cheat, and I'm gonna settle it now!"

"He probably is a lot more than just a cheat," Ki said loudly and clearly.

"You just dug your grave, Chinee."

The bartender looked from Ki to Hollowell. Neither seemed to offer any protest. Cooper lowered his shotgun. "All right, have it your own way." He was resigned to let things follow their own course. "But do it outside."

Tucker's face broadened as his lips peeled back into a vicious, blood-dripping smile. "I'm gonna stomp yer face worse'n a wild stallion."

★

Chapter 9

The crowd gathered outside in the street and formed a large circle. A few of the men held kerosene lamps or placed them around the perimeter of the ring. The combatants didn't need the lamps to see each other, but it allowed the spectators a better view of each blow. No one wanted to miss the punch that would knock out the skinny Chinee.

Tucker rolled up his sleeves ceremoniously. Ki resisted the impulse to strike first with a high *tobi-geri*—a flying kick to the head—though it *was* tempting. He studied his opponent. No matter how stupid he thought Tucker might be, Ki would not make the even more stupid mistake of underestimating his opponent.

"These two babies are going to send you back where you came from, Chinee," Tucker said gleefully as he flexed his mighty arms.

Ki looked at the man's bulging muscles and realized it was no idle boast. Tucker probably had a knockout punch second to none. It would be a rare man who would still be standing after one of those meaty fists connected. The trick then was not to let them connect. But that would be no easy feat. Ki hadn't noticed it before, but Tucker's arms were disproportionate to his size. Tucker had the build, and perhaps, Ki noted dryly, the intelligence of a gorilla. Though Ki was a good deal taller than Tucker, Ki judged his opponent's reach exceeded his own by a good five inches.

Ki continued to circle his opponent warily. But Tucker was having nothing to do with caution. Without further ado, Tucker moved in violently, leading with a powerful roundhouse. Ki sidestepped easily. Tucker came at him again with more determination but no more success.

Ki didn't think he'd have much trouble avoiding Tucker. The man was easy enough to read; his punches started way down from within his boots. All Ki had to do was maintain his distance, although that would not leave him with much of an offense.

"You can run, but you can't hide, Chinee," Tucker said hungrily, then struck out with a left jab.

A quick bob of the head and the fist fell short of its mark. Out of the corner of his eye, Ki saw the knuckles of Tucker's right hand barreling in. His left forearm shot up just in time to stop the crushing blow, but the force of the punch sent him reeling back.

Tucker was on him quickly with another left jab that caught Ki on the side of the face. Ki moved with the punch, and it did little damage, but Tucker was getting awfully close.

"I'm just loosening up a mite on yer ugly yeller face." Tucker's fists were as fast as they were powerful, and his combinations would bear watching. But the man was over-confident, and that would be his undoing.

Ki had seen enough of his fighting style to see how to beat the plug-ugly. Tucker favored his right, setting up the knockout punch with his left jab. But the next time Tucker tried that he would be in for quite a surprise.

After two feints, Ki got his chance. Tucker came out

with a left jab. Ki blocked it, then ducked under the right cross, coming up with two powerful strikes to Tucker's stomach.

Tucker, his breath momentarily knocked out, stumbled back. Ki advanced, but the plug-ugly already had his fists swinging defensively. Tucker gave a little laugh and dropped his fists.

"Come on, " he taunted, "hit me. Hit me hard as you can. Won't do you a lick a good."

Ki suspected he was right. The punches took Tucker by surprise, otherwise they would have had little effect. The man's middle was a thick belt of muscle, solid as sheet iron.

"Maybe you should trade punches with him, Tucker," someone shouted from the crowd.

The comment brought hearty laughter from some, but someone else shouted encouragement to Ki. "Don't be afraid of the dumb ox." Apparently some disliked Tucker enough to want to see him get beat.

"Maybe they should jes' go one for one with each other," suggested another.

Tucker spat at the ground. "Naw, he wouldn't last. What fun'd that be?" Tucker advanced again. But fun was not what he got.

Ki's anger flared. Many a man would settle a disagreement in the streets; it was an accepted way. But Ki disliked the look of pleasure in Tucker's eyes. The man was a sadistic bully. Showing little mercy, he had probably beaten many men to a pulp. But tonight he would learn his lesson.

As Tucker launched his next attack Ki stepped in, spun around, and struck hard with an *empi-uchi* to the solar plexus. With his elbow still pressing into the man's midriff, Ki slammed the back of his fist up into Tucker's face. The man staggered back.

It was Ki's turn to smile. To put maximum power into his *empi-uchi,* or elbow strike, Ki turned away from his opponent and twisted his whole body, elbow first, into the target. As the blow hit, Ki actually had his back to the man. As natural a move as it was to Ki, it was totally disorienting to Tucker. Once Ki pivoted and turned away from him, Tucker didn't know what to expect.

Tucker didn't know what to expect the next time either, or the time after that. Ki repeated the same basic moves, and Tucker still had not caught on how to defend himself. Of course, it was not that easy when your opponent had a range of options. The first time Ki struck with his right elbow; the second time, as Tucker turned to protect himself, Ki swiftly caught him from the other side with his left elbow.

The *empi-uchi* were leaving their mark on Tucker. Muscular as he was, the sharp points of Ki's elbows were causing him to wince in pain every time they connected. They were slowing him down, and Ki found that every elbow strike could be followed with either a back fist or another elbow to the face, and Tucker was virtually unable to defend himself. Most fighters would try at all cost to avoid Tucker's fists, but here Ki was doing just the opposite. He was moving in close—so close that Tucker's fists and long reach were rendered useless.

Ki stepped back and studied his opponent. Barring a lucky shot, and there was always that chance, the fight was over. Tucker was puffing heavily, his face bruised badly. He was beat, but didn't yet know it.

"It takes more than you got, Chinee, to whip me," Tucker hissed in quick gasps. He had barely finished the words before he rushed at Ki, fists flying.

Ki watched carefully, blocked the right hook, and stepped in quickly. Ki and Tucker were standing only a few inches apart. The stocky man was momentarily confused, but not so Ki. In short, rapid strokes Ki pummeled the plug-ugly's face. Though full impact could not be achieved, each fist crashed into Tucker's face with piston-like regularity. The difference between one of Ki's full-force punches and these short jabs was the difference between getting hit with an iron rail or walking into an adobe wall. Though the rail would wield a more devastating wallop, how many times could one walk into a wall? And Ki's fists felt as solid as the thickest adobe.

After more punches than anyone could count, Ki stepped back. Tucker swayed on rubbery legs, but did not fall. His face was battered badly. One eye was swollen and already discolored, and his nose and upper lip fused into one large, bleeding mass of raw flesh. Amazingly, he was still not finished.

"I'm gonna kill you, you bastard. . . ." Tucker wiped at his oozing mouth and looked down at the blood on his hand.

Hollowell eased next to Cooper. "Stop the fight." Cooper pretended not to hear. Even if he had, it would have made no difference.

Suddenly Tucker charged like a maddened bull. Ki noted that, crazed as he was, Tucker still had the wherewithal to keep his face protected from further onslaught. Good. Ki had no further desire to inflict any more punishment. It was time to end the fight.

The second before Tucker's fists would have reached Ki's face, Ki dropped down to his haunches. He brought both fists together, then swiftly swung them up into Tucker's groin.

The man doubled over and bellowed in pain. He hit the ground still screaming loudly and continued to roll in the dirt, his hands holding his crotch. The fight was over. Or at least it should have been.

With herculean stamina, Tucker staggered back to his feet. It was clear he would not give up—not as long as he still had breath left within him.

"Stop the fight," Hollowell repeated loudly.

This time Cooper obeyed. He raised the shotgun into the air and fired the other barrel. "The fight's over for tonight. Everyone back inside." Tucker stared at him blankly. "Go home, Tucker. It's all over."

Tucker didn't seem to comprehend. His opponent was gone, and the crowd was leaving, but he still stood there. Hollowell looked him over. "You got beat, Tucker. Beat bad," he said with disgust, then turned and stepped back into the saloon.

But Ki did not go back to the hotel. Despite the satisfaction he got overhelming Tucker, there was still more to be accomplished.

He hid in the shadows behind the stables and waited for Tucker. He didn't have to wait long before he heard the man drag his feet into the barn.

"Hey, Wes, you old drunk, bring me yer bottle," he shouted angrily.

"Quit yer hollerin'. I ain't so old as I can't hear ya."

Ki crept around to the back door and peeked in.

"Holy mother of mercy!" Wes exclaimed as he came face to face with Tucker.

"Shut up. Get me yer bottle, I said." Wes continued to stare at the man's bloody face. "Keep a staring like that an' you'll be sorry," Tucker snarled as he tossed the bottle he had against the wall. It shattered with a sharp crack.

Wes was too old to argue or defend himself. "I was jes' wonderin' what flight of steps you fell down," he said slyly.

"Never you mind. Now get me that bottle."

Wes walked back to his corner room and returned a minute later with a whiskey bottle. "Now, go easy on that, Tucker. It's my last one till payday," he said as he handed over the whiskey.

Tucker ignored Wes's plea. He uncorked the bottle and took a long swig. "Ain't you got no respect for yer elders?" Wes said with disgust.

"Sure I got respect. I let you live," Tucker answered with a nasty, drunken laugh. "Now saddle up my horse."

"That's my whiskey yer drinkin'. Saddle it yerself."

"I don't got to take any guff from you, old man."

"Look's like you already took more than you can handle. I'm going back to my rocker!" Wes turned and started to walk away.

"Keep walkin' an you'll never make it to the door, old man." Tucker pushed back his shirttail, and his hand dropped to his hip. His sixgun was back in its holster.

Ki tensed and pulled a silver *shuriken* from his pocket. He didn't want to kill Tucker, at least not before the man explained why he had tried to kill the Two Gun Kid, but he wouldn't let him shoot a defenseless man.

Wes turned and looked Tucker square in the eye. "Shoot if ya got the nerve," he said in a strong voice. "But any harm comes to me an' the Kid'll send you straight to hell."

Tucker let out a cocky laugh that fooled no one. "I ain't afraid of the Kid."

Wes gave him a pitying look. "Well, you should be after a beatin' like that."

"The Kid ain't done this to me. He could never lay a hand on me, an' I could outdraw him any day."

Wes turned around and walked back into his room.

"The Two Gun Kid is washed up! He ain't nothin' but an old nag sent out to pasture. If'n he has any smarts he won't be showing his face around here. . . ." He continued to rave; the fact that there was no one to listen bothered him not at all. He staggered over to his mount and with great effort managed to saddle the horse.

The minute Tucker exited the stable Ki raced in and saddled his own horse. He worked smoothly and quickly, and was swinging up into the saddle moments later.

He caught sight of Tucker while the man was still going down the main street. Apparently he was in no hurry, and busied himself more with drinking than riding. Ki followed at a safe distance, but still heard the string of faint curses the man spewed out at an almost constant rate.

It was an easy job of trailing. Though the moon was not yet full, there was a cloudless sky, and enough light to follow Tucker without a problem. There was also the man's gravelly voice and the stink of whiskey that wafted out behind him. Ki was also not burdened by the need for stealth and secrecy. He doubted the man would discover his presence. Ki, by nature, was ordinarily silent, and he knew Tucker would not hear, see, or sense him, especially now. The whiskey—if not the beating—had seen to that.

From the way Tucker held onto the saddlehorn he was obviously having enough of a problem sitting straight in the saddle; turning around was probably far beyond his abilities. Even if Tucker were to turn and stare right down the trail it would be anyone's guess whether the man could see clearly enough to perceive Ki following him.

Ki also cared little whether he was discovered or not. What he had to do he could do as easily along the way as at Tucker's place. Of course he would prefer to trail the man all the way to his abode; there might be an important clue, but in any event he would find out what he had to know.

Ki eased back into the saddle. He didn't know how long a ride it would be to Tucker's place and he might as well relax while he had the chance. During the poker game and the fight Ki had been alert and full of energy. But now, with his mount swaying rhythmically under him, Ki found himself tired. He smiled as he relaxed; if he were involved in an activity that called for strength or vigor, he could easily summon it from his inner resources. But for now he allowed himself the luxury of physical exhaustion.

For a moment he was concerned that his little tussle with Tucker had taken more of a toll than he realized. Had a few weeks of easy living back on the Circle Star made him soft? The thought made him laugh; few people would consider cowboying easy living. After all, Ki had not spent his time sleeping in the shade. There was ranching to be done. But days without combat, days when he didn't have to face a deadly opponent, seemed like days of rest.

Ki thought of that some more. Ranching was not a life without danger. On the contrary, almost every day was filled with a never ending struggle: the struggle of man against nature. And anyone who thought a flash flood, raging brushfire, or sudden tornado did not present a serious foe had probably never faced any of them. Even the more mundane trivialities—scorching heat, blistering rays, or frozen, biting winds offered a good challenge. And cattle drives, Ki thought with a smile, presented their own challenge. A few thousand head of longhorns, spooked by a late-autumn storm . . . a stampede tested a man's courage and ability like perhaps nothing else on this earth.

No, Ki couldn't really call that life relaxing. Save for the fact that he didn't worry as much about Jessie. Mother Nature didn't send up her best to defeat Jessie personally. As much as some ranchers and farmers felt the spirits were purposely turned against them, Ki knew the acts of nature fell equally upon all. Money, prestige, or the lack thereof would not stop a lightning bolt. The wrath of the elements struck with equanimity. Fame and fortune mattered little. When the banks of the river overflowed, everyone got wet.

But greedy men, unlike Mother Nature, chose their targets deliberately. And more often than not, Jessie, in her fight against evil, was the target of vicious killers. While Ki could not be overprotective of her everyday existence —for instance, he would not forbid Jessie to ride a horse simply because the animal, spooked by a snake, might throw and injure her—he could and did protect Jessie from men who sought to bring her harm. It was a full-time job.

These killers lurked everywhere. Wherever Jessie and Ki traveled, whenever they sought to right a wrong, evil men sprang up like worms after a heavy rain. Years ago he had tried to shield Jessie from such dangers; he had once tried to shelter her from confrontations. But he no longer did so. He could not keep her out of the fight any more than he would have tried to stop her father, Alex Starbuck, from pursuing his fight against corruption and evil. She was her father's daughter and had a legacy to fulfill. More than that, Jessie had her own destiny to live out. The fact that Jessie was a woman did not matter—least of all to the men whose evil schemes she had thwarted.

But it mattered to Ki. Or did it? It was a question Ki pondered time and time again. That it was his duty to protect her meant little anymore. His bond was not simply one of duty. There was no doubt he loved the woman—but not because she was female. They shared a bond that transcended the attraction between man and woman. He would have loved the person who was Jessica Starbuck whether she was female or male. Their connection, brother to sister, would be no different brother to brother. But would he worry less if she were a man? Would he be less cautious, less protective? He didn't know, but he doubted it. To be honest, Jessie could take care of herself as well as any man—if not a sight better.

Yet he still wondered about many of his feelings. As perceptive as Ki was, as clearly as he could see the world around him, many of his own feelings remained shrouded behind a veil of mystery. Though deep inside Ki knew the answer. . . .

Ki had been so wrapped up in his own thoughts he wasn't sure when Tucker had fallen silent. For a moment Ki feared he had lost the man, that somehow, somewhere Tucker had slipped off the trail. Ki urged his horse forward. The sky had become cloudy and overcast, and the moon was nothing more than a faint halo behind some high puffy clouds. It was a short gallop before Ki caught sight of his prey. Tucker lay slumped forward in the saddle, his head resting over the mane of his horse. He had had quite a bit more than one drink too many and was peacefully dead to the world. Luckily Tucker's horse was familiar with the route and continued unerringly down the trail. It wasn't long before Ki could make out the outlines of a wooden cabin.

Ki dropped his horse back and approached the cabin with caution. He assumed Tucker lived alone, but he didn't

103

want to take any chances. Sliding down from the saddle, Ki walked silently up to the front door. He was about to peek in through the window when he heard the metallic click of a shell being chambered into a carbine. In the quiet of the night it sounded deathly loud.

Chapter 10

"Hands up, mister, an' turn around real slow."

Ki obeyed. In the darkness, all Ki could see was the figure of a tall man as he stepped out from behind a boulder. From the angle the man approached, Ki could not see the rifle, but he had no doubts it was pointed directly at him.

"You got some talking to do. What d'ya mean sneakin' up on us like that?"

"I was just seeing that Tucker made it home all right," Ki answered quickly. It was ironic that Ki, in his concern over other possible occupants of the cabin, had overlooked the guard. But then why should he have suspected there would be a sentry?

Ki watched the man approach. As long as he kept coming Ki had a chance of disarming him. And if he came close enough to search Ki for a weapon the guard would soon find himself staring down the barrel of the rifle instead of holding the butt. But Ki had to act naturally and answer quickly.

The man looked briefly over to Tucker. "What happened to him?"

"Drunk—and in a fight." Ki took a step toward Tucker.

"Hold it!" the man ordered. "Buck! Buck, wake up an' git yer ass out here."

Ki's hopes fell. There was a good possibility of disarming one man. But disarming two, one of whom had the drop on him, was a risky prospect. Ki decided not to take the chance; there were other ways to get out of this. "Go easy with him, he's pretty banged up," Ki said with much concern.

"I wouldn't be worrying too much about him right now," the guard said threateningly.

The door of the cabin opened, and Buck stepped out into the night. "What's the trouble, Larsen?"

"Caught him sneakin' up on us."

Buck came closer, lit a match, and held it up to Ki's face. "Don't recognize him none. What's yer name, fella?"

"Ki." There was no reason to lie.

"Well, Ki, what's yer business?"

"Just following Tucker home. . . ."

"I don't recall Tucker having no friend by the name of Ki."

"I met him at the saloon." That was, after all, the truth.

Buck walked over to Tucker and lifted his head by the hair. "You do this to him?"

Ki let out a laugh. "Me? No. Two guys I never saw before."

Buck was thinking it over. "What do you think, Larsen?"

"He was sneakin' up on us." The man repeated it as if by rote. "I don't trust nobody who sneaks up in the dark."

Ki wanted to mention that he, himself, didn't trust anybody who stood out at night, rifle in hand, but he kept quiet.

"How 'bout it, Ki?" Buck asked.

"Why'd I go sneaking up on you?" Ki repeated, giving

106

himself another moment to think.

"That's right."

"A man could get shot walking into a cabin in the middle of the night. I figured I'd better have a look first."

"If that don't beat all," Buck said with a laugh. Apparently the man had a sense of irony. "Might be the truth, Larsen. The man ain't packin'."

Ki relaxed slightly. Perhaps his lack of a gun had worked to his benefit, convincing the man to believe his story. But his confidence disappeared as Buck continued.

"Reckon we'll have to wait till Tucker comes round to be sure. No sense shooting a friend of his. We'll just play it safe for now. Cuff him, Larsen."

Larsen stepped forward, but his gun hand lowered slightly as his other hand reached for and pulled out a pair of handcuffs. In this split second, Ki saw his chance. His right leg shot out, caught the rifle barrel, and sent it flying. His leg barely touched down before his other foot snapped sharply into Larsen's chest. The man, caught unawares, tumbled backward into the dirt. And that proved to be Ki's undoing.

He didn't know where the revolver came from. Buck must have had it in the waistband of his jeans; Ki was sure he wasn't wearing a gunbelt. But where it came from was incidental. That it was pointing at him wasn't.

A sharp crack resounded. The bullet kicked up dirt at Ki's feet. "Not another move, Ki." Buck's words held no threat. They didn't have to. All in all the man was not so much threatening Ki as advising him. And Ki knew good advice when he heard it.

Larsen picked himself out of the dirt, retrieved his rifle, and came at Ki a second time. Belatedly, Ki realized that if he had only pulled Larsen into him rather than kicking him away he might have prevented Buck from pulling his gun. At the least, Larsen might have shielded him momentarily from Buck's bullets. But it was too late to brood over past mistakes; he needed to look ahead now.

107

Buck might have been reading his thoughts, for as Larsen grabbed Ki's arms and forced them behind his back Buck spoke out. "He's a tricky one, Larsen. Maybe we best cuff him to one of the cots."

"Good idea."

Buck entered the cabin first. He kept the gun trained on Ki and cautiously maintained his distance. Larsen, feeling confident, poked his rifle into Ki's gut. "Inside, you," he said with a push of the barrel. Ki backed in through the door.

An oil lamp flickered to life. The cabin could have been a line camp of the Circle Star or any other ranch. There were four metal-springed cots, a wood table with two benches, a few wooden shelves stocked with canned goods, and a cast-iron cookstove.

Buck blew out the match and pointed to one of the cots. "Stomach or back?" he asked Ki.

Ki had two quick decisions to make. Handcuffed to the bed, would he have a greater chance of escape if he was facedown, or faceup? And was it really his choice? If Ki picked stomach, would Buck put him on his back? Ki had a hunch the man was being straightforward. He didn't figure Buck to be excessively nasty, so Ki took him at his word. Still, Ki was unsure what would suit him best. "Back," he answered, as he lay down on the cot faceup. All things being equal, he'd just as soon be able to see what was going on around him.

"Sleep better on my back, too," Buck said with a nod.

Larsen took hold of his wrists and pulled them over Ki's head. If he contorted his head back Ki could have watched, but there was no real point to that. He could feel himself being handcuffed to the bed frame. The metal cuffs dug sharply into his wrists, but that was the least of his concerns.

"Almost believed you for a minute, friend," Buck said as he lay down on his own bed. "Until you went after the gun."

Ki suspected Buck wasn't so much making a statement as fishing for more information. "I don't like being confined," Ki answered truthfully.

Buck turned to study him and nodded understandingly. "Well, come tomorrow I may owe you an apology. Then again, I may not. In the mornin' Tucker'll set it straight."

Ki was afraid of just that.

Morning came, but not with sunshine. The sky was gray and featureless. Even without the sun, the day was promising to be a hot one. The air held a sticky dampness that made the heat seem even more uncomfortable. It was the type of day when people just waited for the rain to come and wash away the grime from the back of their necks. It was the type of day when people moved slower, and smiled less.

Jessie was unaware of the gloom around her. She was preoccupied with a conversation in her head—the conversation she planned to have with Sheriff Boswell. She walked briskly, with solid determination, and entered the sheriff's office.

"Mornin', Miss—Starbuck, is it?" Boswell said as he looked up.

"That's right, Sheriff." Jessie sat in the chair opposite his desk.

"What can I do for you today?"

It was a good question. After what the Two Gun Kid had told her, she felt compelled to go to the sheriff. It was the right place to start. But as she faced the pudgy man she wondered about his intentions. Before she would confide what she knew, Jessie wanted to have a better understanding of the man. Just because he was wearing a badge didn't mean he stood for justice.

If Sheriff Boswell was scared of the Two Gun Kid that was one thing. She wouldn't respect him for his cowardice, but cowardice was not necessarily synonymous with being crooked. The sheriff knew his own abilities better than

109

anyone. If he felt going up against the outlaw was suicide, it would be more than cowardice to face the kid; it would be sheer stupidity.

"It's about the murder of Marshal Dixon, and about the Two Gun Kid."

The smile vanished from Boswell's face. "As I told you the last time, I'm working on it. Now you just leave everything to me, and don't worry yer pretty little head over it."

It was the wrong thing to say to Jessica Starbuck. Whatever her mood when she walked in, she was now cross. And when she was cross she was not a woman to be taken lightly. "It's come to my attention that you've been less than diligent in your, ah, investigation."

"I have my own way of working," the sheriff answered calmly.

"Most people think you're just scared of the Kid."

"Most people don't know what the hell they're talking about!"

"That's why I've come to see for myself if you're yellow," Jessie said accusingly.

Boswell's face flushed with anger. "If you'll be so kind as to leave my office now, Miss Starbuck."

Jessie shook her head and remained seated. "Not till I find out what I came for."

"And what is that?"

"If you're yellow or stupid or both." The nastiness of her own words surprised even Jessie. But sometimes a direct confrontation, if not a sit-down, drag-out fight, worked best to get to the bottom of things. Jessie didn't wait for an answer and continued, "I want to know if you think the Two Gun Kid might be innocent, or if you're too scared to arrest the outlaw."

Boswell stared at her, clearly shocked by her verbal onslaught, but he said nothing.

"I want to know if your head is as fat as your bottom," Jessie added as a final touch.

110

Boswell studied her closely. He pulled a cigar from his shirt pocket, struck a match against his boot soles, and leaned back in his chair. His feet slammed down heavily on his desk top. "Ma'am, you sit there 'slong as you like. An' you watch real close." He lit the cigar and sent thick clouds of smoke curling up to the ceiling. "An' when you come to a conclusion you let me know. Cause I'm jus' dyin' to know the very same thing."

Jessie sat there and stared back. Personally she found the man totally irritating. But she was determined not to let her feelings impede her mission. After a suitable length of time had passed, and once she felt there was nothing more to be gained by their stalemate, she spoke out.

"Sheriff, I'm not here to fight you." Boswell blew a large smoke ring. "And I certainly didn't come to insult you."

"Ma'am, you sure had me fooled."

"Eugene was a good friend. I want his killer apprehended. And I'm trying my best to find out who that is." Jessie decided on a new tack. "I'd like us to work together on this," she said, smiling sweetly.

"I'm appreciative of all the help I can get, Miss Starbuck."

Jessie couldn't tell if he was being sarcastic or not. But it didn't matter. "Sheriff, I'd like you to deputize Ki, my associate."

Boswell swung his feet to the floor and leaned over his desk. "I simply can't go around putting a badge on every citizen that wants to help," he explained patiently. "We can't have everybody totin' a gun an' a badge."

"We're not every citizen," Jessie stated simply. "We've worked with the law before on many occasions. With good results, I might add."

"You always get your man." This time there *was* some mockery in his voice.

Jessie ignored it. "That's right, Sheriff. I'm not asking

you to take my word for it. You can contact any U.S. Marshal's office in Texas, or you can contact Marshal Longarm in Denver."

Boswell seemed to study her with a growing respect. "I think I'll do just that right after lunch. But to be honest, Miss Starbuck, I don't know what you hope to accomplish."

Jessie hesitated. She understood why Two Gun couldn't come to the sheriff with his story, but she should be believed, especially after the sheriff checked her references. Still, she felt cautious about letting the cat out of the bag. But then, that was really the reason she had come here in the first place. If worse came to worst the sheriff would simply doubt her story.

"Sheriff, to put it bluntly, I believe that Eugene Dixon was not the intended target of his killer."

The sheriff gave a dry snort. "Well, he did a good job of it . . ."

"I believe the Two Gun Kid was the target."

Boswell shifted uneasily in his chair. "What makes you say that?"

"The outlaw was seen in the saloon, and he was seen leaving. No one saw Eugene leave until he was found shot. I think the killer was lying in wait for the outlaw, not for the marshal." The sheriff looked skeptical. "How would Two Gun know the marshal would be in the alley?"

"I can't answer that," the sheriff said with a shrug.

Jessie could see he was unconvinced. She was purposely leaving out some crucial elements to the story, and she could see how the reasoning was slightly fuzzy. But something seemed odd to her. Contrary to their conversation the other day, Jessie now got the distinct impression that the sheriff did think the outlaw was the guilty one. Was the sheriff simply yellow, and scared of the Two Gun Kid, as everyone seemed to think?

That convinced Jessie to bring up one more point. "Sheriff, why would the Two Gun Kid, clearly the faster draw, have to resort to shooting the marshal in the back? Why not goad him into a showdown and kill him in a fair fight?"

"Wouldn't be exactly what I call a fair fight."

"That's precisely my point, Sheriff."

"Let me think on that some."

"Please do." Jessie stood up to leave.

"An' I'll get back to you after I hear from Marshal Longarm."

"Thank you, Sheriff."

Jessie stepped outside, wondering if she had really accomplished anything. She crossed back to the hotel without reaching a firm conclusion. Before stepping inside she turned around in time to see Sheriff Boswell step out from his office and walk hurriedly down the street. Jessie assumed he was rushing off to the telegraph office and smiled to herself. Had she followed him, though, her smile would have quickly faded.

Boswell went to the stable, and emerged a moment later on a horse, riding hell-bent for leather.

Boswell reined in at the stately mansion that lay about a mile north of the town. The house, a towering structure with ornate cupolas, fancy gingerbread trim, and imported etched glass, would have looked right at home in any of the exclusive neighborhoods of St. Louis, Kansas City, or even Chicago. Here, at the outskirts of Coleville, it stood as a testament to the wealth and power of the owner, Randolph Hollowell. There was not another house like it within a hundred miles. Hollowell had seen to that by carefully destroying anyone whose wealth and power might someday challenge his own authority. Randolph Hollowell had become a very large fish in a small pond. And as the pond grew, so did Hollowell's wealth.

Though it had started that way, his empire did not rest solely on the fortunes of gold, silver, and copper ore found in the mountains. Those were finite; they would not keep a man in power the way Hollowell intended. They were just his starting point. Sensing a need and taking advantage of it, Hollowell founded the Coleville Trust and Loan Company, the area's first bank. Then came the freight company and the telegraph office. By the time the railroad came through, he owned a small piece of that, too. Hollowell expanded into every facet of the growing community. A livery here, a grain store there. Many could not understand why a man like Hollowell would bother himself with penny-ante operations. They assumed it was his miserly, greedy nature. A nickel here, a dime there would eventually add up to a dollar. On volume alone he could grow richer than the average man. But Hollowell craved more than simple wealth; he craved power. With each acquisition he came closer to owning the county and controlling all that lay within.

But Randolph Hollowell was now an old man. He had accountants and lawyers all over the state handling much of his business; but the running of the empire, the day-to-day managing, fell to his son Lewis, or as he liked to call himself, Luke.

Though Luke lacked the drive of his father, he made up for it by being all the more underhanded and shifty. And being primarily lazy, the young Hollowell made things easier on himself by hiring others to do his work. Others, like Sheriff Boswell.

The sheriff dismounted and walked to the side door, where Luke kept his office. He was greeted by a black servant, and escorted into a waiting room. "Mr. Hollowell can't be disturbed right now," the servant informed him. "If you'd kindly wait, sir...."

Boswell never knew whether Hollowell was truly busy or if it was just the man's perverse nature to enjoy keeping people waiting. This wait, though, seemed interminably long. Eventually the servant returned and ushered him into Hollowell's private oak-paneled study.

A few minutes later Boswell walked out, looking trou-

114

bled and unsure. He mounted his horse and rode slowly back to town. He kept rehashing things in his head, and kept coming up feeling like the goat tethered to catch the wolf. But that didn't hold up. Things were still under control. And they could easily be set straight, right now, today. Hollowell was right. If he wanted to run with the stallions he couldn't be afraid to bust out of the barn. Damn that Hollowell! The man held all the cards. Anyway Boswell turned it, he was already in too deep. He knew the way out, but that didn't mean he had to like it. Maybe that damned woman was right. Maybe he was yellow inside. But being right wouldn't do that Starbuck gal a lick of good.

Chapter 11

Sometime in the early hours before dawn, Ki fell asleep. He had been patiently struggling with his bonds, but the handcuffs were not ropes. They did not have any give or stretch. Though Ki tried to contort his hands, he could not slip his wrists past the confines of the metal. Next he tried snapping the chain. He might have been able to do that, but not silently. If he could stand up and place his wrists in front of him, he might get the right leverage, and might be able to put enough chest muscle into the yank to break the chain that held the handcuffs together. With the channeling of his energy and a good "spirit yell," he thought his chances were very good. But he couldn't maneuver his body correctly. With his hands over his head, he could get very little leverage, and he dared not risk a loud *kiai* with Buck asleep and Larsen still standing watch.

So he worked diligently and quietly trying to wear down either the bed frame or the handcuffs. Eventually he wore down his patience. Ki had all the patience in the world, but he also had the intelligence to know when it was useless. He was handcuffed to the bed, and no amount of struggle would change that.

Ki didn't like to admit defeat. He didn't like to think a small hoop of metal could confine him. And most of all, he didn't like to think of the ramifications of that confinement. It didn't require a vivid imagination to know what Tucker would do to him when the plug-ugly woke to find Ki restrained and defenseless. Ki was not a stranger to physical abuse; he had received quite a few beatings—most of which had occurred during his martial-arts training. He had suffered many wounds and injuries, but he had always recovered from them. But there was no doubt in Ki's mind that when Tucker finished with him he would be beyond recovery. As grim as that thought was, there was nothing he could do about it. About the only thing he could do was conserve his energy and strength for when it would serve him best. So Ki closed his eyes and went to sleep.

He woke up briefly when Buck went outside to relieve Larsen, but went right back to sleep. He woke up again in the morning as Larsen stirred awake, but this time he kept his eyes closed and his breathing deep and regular.

"He's still out cold," Larsen said. Ki knew they weren't talking about him. After cuffing him to the bed, they had gone out and carried Tucker inside.

"I don't like it," Buck said.

"Y'mean the Chinaman?" There was no answer, but Ki heard someone get up. He could feel the face that bent down and studied him.

"Don't mind him, Buck. He's sleeping like a log."

"I don't like the whole thing."

"The Chinaman?" Larsen persisted. There was no answer. "You think it was the Kid?" he continued.

"Can't say. But I don't figure it that way. If the Kid knew what Tucker done, Tucker'd be lying there with more holes in him than he's got bruises."

"Yeah. Do you think the Kid'll ever find out?"

"Don't matter to me none. He gets what he deserves. . . ."

"If he had pulled it off right in the first place, he wouldn'ta had to worry about the Kid a'tall. But I kinda like it that he done poorly at it." Larsen chuckled to himself. "Gives us a chance to have some fun and blame it all on the Kid."

"I guess some good'll come from it. But I don't like it."

"You'll like that sweet young thang all right. Oooeee, will you like it. Lord, I could do with some right now! An' it all gets blamed on the Kid. Oooeee!"

"Larsen, you're gonna get that neck of yers stretched good."

"Aw, Buck, don't get yer dander up. If yer partial to the old widow just say so. I'll take the young filly, an' you kin take her mom."

Ki felt a wave of almost uncontrollable fear sweep through him. Even without names he knew they were talking about Nell and Katie Dixon. Coupled with that fear was Ki's intense frustration. He knew the two women were in mortal danger, yet there was nothing he could do to protect them. But somehow, somehow he knew he must. . . .

"Shut up, Larsen. We were hired to rustle some cattle, an' stir up trouble."

Larsen laughed. "We sure done just that," he said gleefully.

"No better way to bring the law down on us than to start killin' folks right an' left."

"The law or the Kid?" Larsen asked pointedly.

"What's the difference? They can both get the job done. Dead is dead!"

"You ain't getting soft, are ya, Buck?"

"Jus' smart. It ain't worth a few weeks' drinkin' money. We ain't getting more than that. If'n I'm gonna risk my life

I'll do it holdin' up a bank. I ain't doin' this to make some rich dude richer."

"I think you are soft. And I think it is the Kid."

Buck didn't argue. "Call it what you like. But when Collins gets back with the boys, I'm kickin' up the dust."

"Collins ain't gonna take kindly to you leavin'."

"That's his problem," Buck said tersely.

Ki began to feel that there might be a chance. If he could talk to Buck alone, perhaps he could convince the man to set him free.

"Well, I think I'll take a swim before it rains. Damned hot!"

That was Larsen talking. Ki's hopes sprang up, then died.

"I'll come with you."

The two men left. Ki opened his eyes and stretched. It was then that it hit him. He didn't have to free himself from the handcuffs; he just had to have the use of his hands. It was so simple Ki wondered why he hadn't thought of it sooner. But then he quickly realized that he did think of it the very moment the opportunity presented itself. There was no point concocting a strategy that was not applicable. His plan was feasible only if and when he was left alone. And now he was alone. It might work. . . .

It was not as contradictory as it sounded. His hands were cuffed to the bed, which in turn restricted his whole body. His confined position also restricted the use of his hands. But his hands had some freedom of movement, as did his body. The trick would be to shift one to maximize the freedom of the other.

The clue had come while he was stretching. It was simple, and in theory it should work. But could Ki flip his legs over his head and wind up in a kneeling position facing the bed without tearing his arms from their sockets or dislocating his shoulder? He tested it tentatively, but there was only one way to find out. Ki was arching his back and

119

preparing to flip his legs over when he broke out into a huge grin.

He was still smiling broadly when he rolled off the side of the bed and onto his knees. It took him a few maneuvers as he twisted around to the front of the bed. It always amazed Ki how the solutions to many problems could be so easily found once he stopped trying to fight against the forces and worked with them instead. Instead of using his energy to fight the restriction, he simply worked around it.

Ki lifted up the metal cot and dragged it over to Tucker. Larsen was right, the man was still out cold. That would make it even easier. Ki was able to move his hands a few inches, but more importantly, he was able to grab things with his fingers. He pulled out Tucker's revolver.

He now had two options. But after some serious contorting and bending of his hands, head, and chin, Ki gave up on the first option. There was no way he could hold the gun and fire it at the chain that held the two cuffs.

Ki dragged his cot slightly behind the head of Tucker's. After trying a considerable number of positions, Ki found one that enabled him to train the gun either at Tucker's head or at the door of the cabin. But it was not a comfortable position. Ki was kneeling on his right knee, not in itself a difficult posture to maintain, but the bed had to be twisted at an odd angle and was held up and out of the way by his wrists and left thigh. Ki didn't know how long he would be able to maintain this position. Then he thought of Katie at the hands of Larsen and he knew he would manage as long as he had to.

Fortunately Ki did not have to wait long. At least it didn't seem long. His mind was set with an iron determination, and where his mind went his body followed. His attention was so focused, his body would have remained steady all day, if not longer.

The door swung in. Ki quickly turned his wrists to the left. The revolver was pointed right at the back of Tucker's head.

"Move and he's dead." Ki reacted by reflex. But as he took a look at the man in the doorway he realized he had made a mistake.

Larsen stood there, a look of surprise frozen on his face. "Take it easy, fella." Though he was careful not to move his body, his face slowly spread into a huge grin.

Ki should have known then what would follow. Afterward he wondered if he had purposely challenged the man. No, he couldn't really call it a challenge. Larsen acted of his own accord, or rather, of his own stupidity.

"There's no need to get itchy with that finger," Larsen said cautiously. "I know what you want. . . ."

Right then Ki should have switched the gun to Larsen. He had seen enough of the man's personality to know Larsen cared little for other men's lives. But Ki thought he heard Tucker stir. If Tucker were about to wake, it would be best to keep the gun exactly where it was. But maybe Ki was remembering what Larsen would do if he got the chance to call on Katie and Nell Dixon. . . .

"I want the keys to the cuffs," Ki said calmly.

"Sure, fella . . . they're in my pocket. I'm gonna slide my hand down real easy-like."

Afterward Ki wondered if things would have happened differently had he asked Larsen to throw down his gun first, then reach in for the keys. Probably not.

"Don't move, Tucker, he got a gun at yer head," Larsen said nervously. It was a shrewd move. It might have worked with another man, but not with Ki. Ki's attention was riveted on Larsen's hand: slow-moving and steady, then a blur as it reached for his gun.

How did the fool think he could outdraw a man who already had his gun out? Ki would never know the answer. He swiveled his wrists in a small arc and shot Larsen down.

Tucker struggled to a sitting position. Was the plug-ugly really awakening, had Ki been correct in thinking the man was stirring; or did the booming gunshot, just inches from

121

his ear, wake him? Those were questions Ki would never know the answers to.

Ki acted quickly, bringing his wrists down hard on the man's head. Ki didn't know whether it was his hands, the grip of the gun, or the bed frame that delivered the major impact of the blow. All that mattered was that Tucker was again out like a doused lamp.

Ki moved quickly, bed frame in tow, to Larsen's fallen body. Surprisingly, the man still breathed. They were shallow, irregular breaths, but the man was clinging to life. Ki dug his hands into the man's pocket, but the pocket was deeper than the freedom of his cuffs allowed. Ki pulled his hands out, and with a swift tug ripped the cloth. The pocket tore away and the key to the handcuffs fell to the floor.

The next few moments were the most dangerous of the whole plan. In order to free himself, Ki had to hold the key in his mouth and twist his wrists over backward to get access to the keyhole. It was, to say the least, a very vulnerable position. If Buck were to walk in now there would be no defense. Although it would only take a few seconds, it took less time than that to put a bullet into a man's head.

The thought helped Ki to work quickly. The first cuff opened smoothly, and the second fell to the floor only a second later.

He rubbed his wrists briefly, then turned his attention to Larsen. The man's breathing was even fainter now, and seemed to become more so with each labored breath. At this close range the .44 had made a nice-sized hole in the man's gut. Ki lifted him up and saw the even larger hole between the man's shoulder blades. There was no hope for him. The bullet had passed through the vital organs and then traveled up and out through the lungs. Ki lowered him back to the floor.

Larsen's eyes were open, but he was unaware of the world around him. He would be gone from it in a matter of a minutes, if that long. Ki felt no remorse. Though it was a

122

senseless, unnecessary killing, Katie and countless other young women would sleep better for it.

Ki picked up Tucker's gun and, with the revolver leading the way, he stepped outside. At the same instant Buck turned the corner of the cabin and came face-to-face with Ki.

No words were necessary. Buck knew exactly what to do. He raised his hands high into the air.

"Larsen?"

"Dying." There was no surprise on Buck's face. But Ki felt a need to explain. Whether he did so as a warning—a word to the wise—or as a common courtesy, he wasn't sure. "He was a fool, Buck. I had the drop on him, but—"

"I know the type of man he was." There was just the slightest trace of sorrow in his words.

"Drop your gun," Ki ordered. "Left hand, two fingers."

"Don't worry 'bout me, friend. I'm no fool." Unlike Larsen his words were not meant as a distraction. He did just what he was asked.

"Good. I really don't want to have to shoot you." Ki meant it. Ever since Buck gave him the choice of "stomach or back," he had liked the man. Though he was an outlaw, he had a sense of fair play and honesty that Ki respected.

"That makes two of us," Buck said with a smile. He seemed to relax some, knowing that his life was not in immediate danger.

"Inside." Ki motioned with the gun.

On the floor, Larsen was dead. Ki bent down and picked up his revolver. Tucker was still out on the cot. Ki smiled at Buck. "Sit tight and you'll live to see old age."

"Like I said, I'm no fool. An' I got no bone to pick with you, or the Kid. I'll bury Larsen, then I'm off on the wind."

Ki did not doubt him. There was nothing more that had to be said. Ki was backing out the door when Buck called out after him.

"Give the Kid my how-do. . . ."

Ki nodded and closed the door.

He wondered why or how Buck suspected he was aligned with the Two Gun Kid. Ki even thought to deny any association with the outlaw, but there was no point. By the next day, Buck would be gone in a cloud of dust.

Ki untied the two horses, mounted one, then gave the other a good slap on the rump. With a loud hoot he was down the trail and soon out of sight.

A half-mile down he pulled the horse off the trail. When he came to a low-lying gully he dismounted and tethered the animal to a scrub elm. The site was well hidden by a row of thickets. Even if someone were to wander off the trail he wouldn't see the horse till he was almost upon it.

Ki hiked to the trail, then doubled back to the cabin. Though he didn't believe Buck would come looking for him, he didn't know when Collins, the rustler boss, and the other boys might be returning, so he took the precaution of staying out of sight.

He circled around the cabin, coming up on it from behind. Off to the right he could hear the sounds of digging: Buck burying Larsen. Lying in the bushes Ki was well concealed and didn't have to fear being discovered, but he didn't have a very good view of the front of the cabin. He listened closely, debating whether to move while Buck was still hard at work, or wait till he had finished the job. He decided to change his position now. As long as he heard the digging he knew where Buck was. Once Buck stopped working Ki couldn't be sure of the man's whereabouts. There also were other reasons that convinced Ki the time to move was now. First, the sounds of the digging would hide whatever slight sounds Ki might make, and as long as Buck was occupied he would be less likely to be looking around. Most people concentrated on the ground as they worked a shovel. That would suit Ki perfectly.

Ki hurried from behind the bushes and raced over to the corner of the cabin, where a large oak stood. One moment he was standing next to the trunk, the next he was well concealed among the top foliage. Even if someone were to look straight up it was doubtful he would see the man nestled in among the branches.

High up in the tree Ki was cool and comfortable. He also had a commanding view of the area. He noticed for the first time the small meadow that stretched out behind the cabin. Tucked in between two low hills, it was well sheltered from the elements and the prying eyes of man.

It came as no surprise when he saw a small, distant cloud of dust rise up from the other side of the hill. It did not take much to guess what that was.

An hour or so later, the first head of cattle—no doubt stolen—were driven into the meadow. Buck, who had been sitting outside the cabin, walked down to meet them.

Hours of waiting had been for nothing. Ki had assumed that when Collins returned, he would ride up to the cabin. From his perch Ki was hoping to overhear some bit of conversation that would tie a lot of loose ends together and ultimately point out the man responsible and the reasons for Marshal Dixon's murder.

But in all probability, whatever information was to be imparted would take place in the meadow, far out of Ki's earshot.

He briefly considered sneaking down after Buck, but dismissed it as suicidal. Besides being outnumbered, Ki wouldn't have any cover down at the field.

Ki was going to wait just a little longer, but when he saw the men head for the stream that ran along the base of the far hill, he decided it was time to go. He didn't get a close look at any of the men, but Ki had a feeling their identities were not crucial to solving the Dixon murder. And there was something else of importance to attend to.

He had taken a gamble, though a very slight one, by postponing his mission. But there was little more to gain by remaining here, and Ki did not like to take unnecessary risks with other people's lives. Especially when they were as sweet and sexy as Katie Dixon.

Ki would by no means consider Larsen a unique thinker. He was a cheap rustler and gunman who thought little of the sanctity of life. And the other men down by the stream were probably not all that different from Larsen. If Larsen realized the possibility of committing more crimes and pinning the blame on the Two Gun Kid, others would think of it too. Just because Larsen was dead didn't mean Nell and Katie Dixon were safe from harm. To a man, Larsen's compadres were sure to be as lustful and brutal as he was.

★

Chapter 12

Jessie knocked on the door impatiently, but she knew it was pointless. If the sheriff were in, the door would be open. But the door was locked. Jessie could bang on it all she wanted and it wouldn't matter.

Surely he should have received a return cable by now. But when the sheriff didn't come round to the hotel, Jessie decided to pay him another visit in his office.

She started down Main Street, intent upon the telegraph office. Midway there she changed her mind. She doubted the operator would give her any information. She turned around, but then changed her mind once again. To a casual observer, she would seem to have been stricken by the heat. Why else would a woman spin on her heels, turn completely around, and then continue on her way as if nothing had happened?

But Jessie was feeling anything but sickly. On the slim chance that a young man was working in the telegraph office Jessie decided to give it a shot. It wasn't that she would try anything immoral. She would never use her feminine wiles to lure an innocent victim. But she did find that young, good-looking men were often slightly more eager to please her. Her questions wouldn't be illegal, but she knew a hard-line, rigid man would not be too accommodating.

She entered the telegraph office and a stern man in his late fifties looked up from the desk. Jessie's first impulse was to turn and walk out, but since he had already asked if he could help her, she decided to try anyway.

"Yes. My name is Jessica Starbuck. I'm expecting a cable from Marshal Longarm, Denver. I wonder if it's come in yet."

"Nothing, ma'am."

"It might have come in for Sheriff Boswell."

"You'd have to take that up with him, ma'am."

"He sent the message out for me earlier today, I'm not sure exactly what time. . . ."

There was no response from the telegrapher—no sign that could be read either way. She'd give it one more shot.

"He's not in his office now, so I thought maybe you could help me. . . ."

"Sorry, ma'am, nothing came in for Starbuck. As for the sheriff, you'd have to ask him. Company rules."

"Thank you anyway."

She expected as much. Jessie was half tempted to send a cable to Denver herself. Marshal Longarm could answer her question easily enough, but by the time she got a response it wouldn't matter. Though she hadn't learned anything specifically she had the growing suspicion that Boswell had never sent a cable in the first place.

Back on Main Street she walked to the other end of town and dropped in at the stable to see how Wes was getting on. Wes was glad to see her and started to get her horse.

"I don't need my horse, Wes. I'm not heading out." She could see the question coming. "I'm waiting for the sheriff, an' just thought I'd mosey over to say hello."

128

Wes looked even more puzzled. "He got back some time ago, Jessie."

That puzzled her, too. But then suddenly Jessie was overcome by a wave of fear. Not for herself, but for Two Gun. It made no sense, there was no reason to it, but nonetheless she was terrified for the outlaw who lay sleeping in her bed.

She raced out of the barn, leaving an even more confused Wes.

Jessie bounded up the hotel stairs two at a time. At the landing she stopped cautiously. She was just turning the corner when a figure stepped out of the far end of the hall. The man was coming from the stairs that went up into the attic.

"Miss Starbuck," the voice said ominously. It had a familiar ring to it.

Jessie barely had time to answer before the shots rang out. They came from behind her, booming loudly in the confined space. She spun around to look, but out of the corner of her eye she saw a man stagger backward and tumble over the banister. She turned back around in time to see the body fall to the floor of the lobby. It hit with a loud thump. Sheriff Boswell lay there faceup—and dead.

The Two Gun Kid stepped out of the shadows, both Peacemakers smoking. "Are you all right?" he asked softly.

Stunned, Jessie nodded. She couldn't believe Two Gun had just killed the sheriff.

Below them, a woman was screaming.

"No one move or I'll shoot her," the outlaw warned loudly. Jessie noticed that both guns were pointed directly at her.

Two Gun studied the crowd that formed below. His eyes moving constantly as he slowly backed into Jessie's room.

Jessie still couldn't believe what she had just seen. She turned to run down the stairs, and then suddenly everything

129

made sense—at least partial sense. In the wall behind her head was a fresh bullet hole. Boswell had tried to shoot her! The Two Gun Kid had saved her life.

She raced down the stairs and pushed her way to the sheriff. "Quick, someone get a doctor," she yelled frantically. Bending over the body, she saw he had been shot twice through the heart. Or at least where his heart had once been. And it was only an educated guess that he had been hit by two bullets. There was only one wound visible, but it was of a larger diameter than one piece of lead would have made.

"Hurry, I think he's still alive! Someone get the doctor!" she wailed hysterically. It was an outright lie. The only man Boswell needed was an undertaker. But she wanted to create as much confusion as possible. Maybe she could buy Two Gun enough time to slip away.

She looked up at her room and really poured it on. "Don't go in there," she screamed at no one in particular, though it was doubtful anyone would try. "He's a killer . . . he's just waiting for someone to go in there. He's just waiting to shoot someone," she wailed.

As it turned out, with an outlaw like the Two Gun Kid her hysterics were unnecessary. There wasn't a man in the room who was even thinking of going up the stairs. The Kid's reputation, and his proven skill with a gun, were enough to keep anyone from wanting to play the hero. And with the sheriff dead it would be a while before a posse would be organized.

Jessie saw the doctor push his way through the crowd. She stood up and let herself get pushed to the rear as people edged in around her. A moment later she was out the back door.

For a moment it all seemed so familiar. For the second time she stood in the alley and looked for signs of a fleeing man. Like the other time, she found none. Beyond that nothing else was the same, but it gave her an idea.

She was not able to climb up onto the rear overhang as easily as the intruder had climbed down, but she did manage it.

From the corner of the second-floor hall, she heard, though she couldn't see, the commotion that was still going on in the lobby. Jessie had to get into her room, and if she could do it unnoticed that would be all the better. She tried to ease her nerves by telling herself that Two Gun had already gotten away and it didn't matter. She also told herself no one would look up, and even if they did they might not realize what she was doing till it was too late.

With a deep breath, she calmly walked down the hall. Thank goodness the door was not locked. Quickly, she ducked into her room and closed the door swiftly but silently behind her.

Jessie slipped the bolt closed, then turned to study the room. She was hoping Two Gun had left her a note. But she didn't see anything. With a sinking heart, she wondered if the outlaw could even write. But then, looking around the room, she realized there was nothing to write with. Also, if there were a clue it would not be that obvious. The Kid would not leave behind something that could be found by others. Jessie searched the bed and the closet, but to no avail.

Suddenly she thought she had it. She went back to the closet and reached up to the shelf where she kept her Colt .38. It was missing, or so she thought. As she turned around she saw the gun sitting on top of the dresser. As she picked up the gunbelt she saw faint tracings outlined in the thin dust film that covered the dresser top. She studied the line drawing; it could definitely be a simple map. She immediately memorized the pattern, then wiped the dresser clean with her shirtsleeve.

Jessie strapped on her gun, stepped over to the window, and looked down. It was not that great a drop. If Two Gun, bandaged and still healing, could do it, she could do it. She crawled through the opening, and then, hanging down from the windowsill, she dropped the twelve feet to the ground.

This time she had Wes saddle her horse. As he brought the bay out to her, she asked him casually how far it was to the fork in the main road.

"The one headin' out to Humbolt County?"

"Is there another fork?"

"Not that I know of."

"Then that's the one."

"'Bout five miles."

"And is there another road that crosses it farther up?" Jessie was picturing the lines on her dresser.

"Not for another ten miles or so there ain't."

She didn't picture the map to be on that large a scale. "Maybe an old wagon trail?" she wondered out loud.

"Lotsa old trails through here, Jessie. Could be."

That wasn't much help. It was even possible that Jessie wasn't interpreting the lines correctly. She had assumed the straight line that ran the length of the diagram was the main road running through town. Now that she knew a major fork existed she took the other lines to be intersecting roads or paths.

Wes studied her curiously. "What exactly you lookin' for, Jessie?"

"I'm not sure," she said in all honesty.

"Then I'm 'fraid I can't be much help."

"You've already helped more than you realize." She took the reins of the horse. "One more questions, Wes—which way?"

The man wore the most puzzled expression, but he pointed north. "Thataway."

Jessie swung up into the saddle and was about to thank him for the help when something in his eyes changed her mind. Wes was one of the few men in this town she thought she could trust. He also had a self-admitted liking for the Kid. Jessie didn't want to compromise the outlaw's safety, but maybe there was something else Wes could tell her.

She leaned over the neck of the horse. "Wes, is there an abandoned farmhouse or ranch out that way?"

Wes moved closer. "What exactly are ya lookin' for, Jessie?" he repeated again, but this time there was an edge to his voice.

"A good rendezvous point. A spot that wouldn't be too well-known, maybe someplace to lie low. . . ." She couldn't say any more.

Wes scratched at his face. "There is an old abandoned gristmill out on Watson Creek."

"Of course!" Jessie exclaimed. That intersecting line, the one she thought was a winding trail, was actually a stream.

"The Kid used to do some fishin' out thataways, long, long, time ago."

Jessie smiled broadly. "Looks like a good day for some fishin', Wes."

"The bass bite well on rainy days," he said in all seriousness.

"Thanks, Wes," she said sincerely as she straightened up in the saddle.

"An' if'n you see any friends o' mine, give 'em my best."

Jessie gave a wave and a smile as she urged the horse on its way.

She kept the horse at a walk until she hit the end of town, then spurred it into a full gallop.

At the fork she dismounted and looked for signs. Not so much to verify that Two Gun has passed this way, but to be sure other horses—a posse—had not.

She found one set of fresh prints, and though she couldn't identify them she was certain they belonged to Two Gun's mount. There were no other fresh prints. She remounted feeling much better. Jessie knew that it was unlikely a posse would have formed so quickly and already been hot on his trail, but ever since she had left town something had bothered her. If Wes knew some of the Kid's hideaways, perhaps someone else, less amiable toward the outlaw, would also be able to trace him to the deserted mill.

A few miles down the road she came to Watson Creek, or what was left of it. It was no wonder the mill had been abandoned. From the tree growth she could make out that the creek had once been a wide and probably fast-flowing stream. Large weeping willows stood opposite each other about twenty-five yards apart. That would have marked the two edges of the stream. But now secondary growth had filled in the sandy bottom. The small shrubs grew up to the watermark, now only a few feet wide at most.

She followed the creek upstream, finding more signs that once this had been a larger stream. She wondered whether or not the stream had died a natural death. She ruled out drought almost immediately. There was too much growth to imagine a dry season, or even two or three had been responsible. Perhaps there was a man-made dam farther upstream. Sometimes a landowner would reroute a waterway to irrigate fields or pastures, but she ruled that out. Not with a mill farther downstream. Damming the water would mean instant disaster for the mill and its owner. Most likely there was some natural cause. A rockslide somewhere near the source, or even simple erosion, could have changed the course of the stream.

Most likely Jessie would never find out, but she was interested nonetheless. Land was the real wealth, whether you were mining gold from the mountains or planting seed in the soil. The land was the essence of it all. Every head she sold at market owed its existence to the land. They grazed on it, drank from it. It paid to keep a keen eye on changes that occurred.

Even people who realized the value of land often became sloppy and careless. After all, there seemed to be an abundance of it. Even good land was not necessarily scarce. But good land did not always remain so. This stream with its abandoned mill was a case in point. A pasture overgrazed would be useless for the next few seasons. Only so much could be taken from each square foot; there was only so much that would grow. Too many cattle, too many sheep would wear a field down till it was nothing but weeds, rocks, and dust. To many of the rich ranchers that didn't matter; there was always another hundred acres, and another, and another. But the small spreads had to be careful. They didn't have the resources to expand indefinitely, especially now that most of the open range was gone.

It was ironic that pastures on the open ranges tended to last longer. Cattle weren't herded according to any artificial boundaries that marked one rancher's land from another's. Herds tended to graze where the growth was more plentiful, giving the more worked fields a needed rest and time to repasture. But it seemed the men who were putting up fences were also the men who would abuse the land more. That had never quite made sense to Jessie. If she owned something she'd give it extra care, and try all the harder to keep it in good condition. But many large ranches, especially the newer conglomerates, tried to squeeze as much from the land as they possibly could.

Initially, Jessie had suspected that was due to ignorance. Many spreads were now owned by wealthy absentee owners. A Kansas City banker or San Francisco shipping merchant couldn't be expected to know the finer points of ranching. They couldn't understand the land the way the people who lived on it did. She figured in time they would learn. But she was wrong.

It was not a question of ignorance, it was one of priorities. This new breed of landowner put profits first, above everything else. They could afford to. They didn't have to face the more immediate question of survival. But Jessie remembered a time (even if some of it was actually before her time), when ranchers cared nothing for turning a profit.

135

They wanted only to make it to the next season. They wanted to have enough food for their families. They wanted enough livestock to make it through the winter. They wanted to survive another Indian attack. Survive, survive, survive. That was everything. Profits were something that would happen next fall—honest. The next roundup would turn a profit, really. More calves would be born and, come spring, there'd be an excess of money. That's the way it used to be. But times were changing. And times could destroy a man as easily as times could dry up a river.

Lost in her thoughts, Jessie was surprised to find it was raining. It was a gentle rain, almost a heavy mist. She raised her head and studied the sky. It was a thick, solid gray, but it was impossible to guess whether the light rain would continue falling or turn into a major storm.

As she lowered her gaze she saw the outline of the old mill. The top floor, built of planking, had burned down years ago, but the foundation of fieldstone remained solid. The broken-down waterwheel stood several feet above the sandy dirt. It reminded Jessie of a wrecked paddlewheeler. It not only looked out of place, but it also appeared very depressing against the lifeless gray backdrop.

Then, from behind the rock foundation, out stepped the Two Gun Kid.

Jessie sent the horse flying ahead, and was soon swinging down next to the Kid.

"I'm glad you found it," he said with a warm smile.

"Are you all right?" Jessie studied his head bandage.

"Fine. A little sore, but that's all."

"No bleeding?" Jessie was worried that his wounds would have reopened with all the activity.

"Nope. Tight as a Wells Fargo box," he said with a smile. But the smile faded as his voice turned serious. "Jessie, I don't know why I left you that map. . . ."

"I'm glad you did. That was very clever."

"I think I just wanted to explain. I don't want you

thinkin' I gunned the sheriff down like that."

Jessie quickly understood what was troubling him. "Two Gun, I understand almost everything. I should be thanking you for saving my life."

"How did you know?" he said with surprise.

"The bullet hole in the wall next to my head."

"The sheriff's."

Jessie nodded. "If you were a second slower I wouldn't be standing here. But how did you know!"

"That Boswell was gunning for you?"

Jessie nodded.

"I didn't. I had to, ah, well, you know, ah . . ."

"I understand," she said, smiling over his embarrassment to discuss such things with a lady.

Two Gun returned the smile, grateful to be off the hook. "Anyway, I was coming back, through the rear window, of course—"

"Of course."

"—when I heard someone coming up the stairs. I ducked behind the corner. The footsteps stopped and there was a knock at the door. Your door. Of course there was no answer; we were both out. Funny thing is, I didn't hear footsteps going back down the stairs."

"So you waited at one end of the hall while the sheriff waited at the other."

"'Cept I didn't know it was the sheriff then. When I heard him call your name, I stepped out. You saw the rest."

"I wouldn't exactly say that. Don't get me wrong, Two Gun, but your reputation is well deserved." So she wouldn't be misunderstood, she added quickly, "That was a fine piece of shooting." Somewhat to his credit, Jessie noted he seemed to take little pleasure in the compliment. "You always take your guns with you when you—"

"I take 'em everywhere," he answered quickly.

"I'm glad you do. Thank you." She leaned forward to give him a kiss. It was going to be an innocent peck on the lips, but when Two Gun's arms came around her and pulled her close the innocence was gone.

Jessie pressed her lips hotly against his. Her body seemed to melt against the outlaw as his warm breath filled her mouth. With his tongue snaking its way inside her mouth she felt tremors run along her spine. Jessie didn't remember closing her eyes, but she opened them with a start as she felt herself slipping away. Was she really swooning or was it her imagination? But there was nothing unreal about the man who held her tight.

"Jessie, I think I know now why I wanted you to follow me so badly," he whispered in her ear. "I had to hold you like this, at least once." His lips returned to hers, and they kissed passionately once again.

Suddenly she was overcome by a deep longing. From out of nowhere she recalled the first night she had nursed Two Gun. How inviting his body had seemed. How manly he had looked against the white sheets, how muscular, how thick and throbbing he was. It took her a minute to realize that it wasn't her imagination stirring; it was Two Gun's body pressing against hers. That was not her memory she felt poking out from between his legs.

And still their mouths pressed against each other, their tongues dancing, exploring. Jessie pulled back. "Let's go inside," she whispered.

Two Gun hesitated momentarily.

"Let's at least get out of the rain," Jessie said with a giggle.

The Kid shook his head. "Not now, Jessie. Not because I don't want you. But it's not safe. Not here, not now."

"I understand," she said regretfully. She was worried about that herself. "By the way, Wes sends his greetings . . ."

"Wes?" he said, confused.

Jessie nodded. "He seemed to think you'd be here—fishing."

138

"He would, the old coot." But it was not said without affection.

"Others might know, too?" Jessie wondered out loud.

"Maybe, maybe not. The old mill isn't a secret. But there is a place where we can be safe."

"And then . . . ?" she cooed enticingly.

"And then we can take all the time in the world."

"I hope you're a man of your word, Two Gun."

"There's not many that'll call me a liar to my face."

He said it with a smile, but after his skilled display back in the hotel, Jessie realized there was an icy edge to the joke.

Chapter 13

As they started out, Jessie was concerned that the wet ground would leave distinct prints that would be easy to follow. After a short distance she voiced her opinion, but Two Gun told her not to worry.

"If anyone tracked us to the mill they'd be sure to find us, wherever we're going," Jessie said in protest.

Two Gun smiled gently. "Unless the rain washes out all the trails."

Jessie stuck out her hand, palm up. She looked dubious. "Not a gentle rain like this."

"I haven't seen a 'gentle rain' in these parts that didn't turn into a real whopper of a summer storm," he answered confidently.

"I hope you're right." Jessie turned her thoughts to another matter. There was still something that didn't make sense—something that didn't fit in no matter how she looked at it.

"Two Gun, why do you think the sheriff came gunning for me?" she asked eventually.

"Can't say."

"No idea?"

"None."

Then it struck her. It wasn't the answer, but maybe it would point to it. "Earlier in the day, I went and had a talk with him. I told him what you told me."

Two Gun reared in his horse and turned to face Jessie. "You told him about the marshal?" he accused sharply.

"I left out certain details," she said just as sharply. "Basically I told him my investigation led me to believe you were the target, not Dixon. But I didn't say anything about you and the marshal."

That eased Two Gun some, but he still didn't seem pleased.

"Does that help you reason this thing out better?" Jessie persisted.

"Let me think on it a bit," he said simply, then started his horse down the trail again.

Not long after that the first crack of thunder sounded in the distance. The rain started to get heavier, and before long the two riders were soaked to the bone.

Jessie pulled her horse alongside the Kid's. "You don't have to say I told you so," she said with a smile.

"What?"

"I said I hope it's warm and dry where we're heading."

"It is," the outlaw said flatly.

"We almost there?"

"Nope."

That was just what Jessie wanted to hear. There was nothing she liked better than a long ride through the pouring rain with a sulking, angry man. Even if that man did have a kiss that would send shivers down her spine.

A few minutes later, Two Gun turned around. "Jessie, I'm not so much mad at you as I am at myself. I'd hate to think that you might have gotten killed because of me."

"I understand." She really did; she had felt the same way herself, worrying often that friends' lives were sometimes endangered simply by their association with her. She wanted to say more to show Two Gun that she really did understand and was not just saying so, but he was already moving on.

"See that peak there?" he said, pointing to the horizon. "We're headin' 'bout eight miles shy of that."

Jessie followed his finger. "I thought those were clouds." The difference between the jagged gray mountain and the ragged gray sky was almost nonexistent. It was impossible for Jessie to judge the distance. "How far?" she asked.

"Another two hours."

"Let's cut that in half," she yelled and sent her horse into a gallop.

A few miles later Two Gun slowed his horse to a walk. "If I knew you could ride that well we could have shaved off even more time."

"There are lots of things I can do well."

Two Gun's eyes lit up.

"That's not what I meant," she said with a smile, "but I can do that well, too."

The woods gradually enveloped them, growing denser as they progressed farther into the high country The rain, still heavy, had a soft, muted sound as it came falling through the green boughs. The ground underneath, a thick carpet of loam and moss, muffled the pounding of the animals' hooves. Jessie couldn't shake the sensation of gliding through an underwater paradise. The filtered light, the sweet smell of pine, and water everywhere—streaming past her eyes, down her cheeks, against her breasts. This ride through the forest, with its lush shades of green and enticing aromas, should have been peaceful and serene. But not when she was wet, chilled, and her teeth were chattering. If only she had an oilskin slicker.

Appearing almost out of nowhere a solid wall of granite rose up in front of them. They turned and followed it for about a half-mile, then Two Gun stopped and dismounted.

"It's usually easier to lead your horse through."

"Through what?" Jessie wondered aloud.

Two Gun smiled. "You'll see."

He took his horse by the bit and started for the base of the granite cliff. Jessie slid down from her saddle and followed. It was rough going. There was a thirty-yard stretch of boulder field to traverse that would have been difficult in any weather, but in the heavy rain the rocks were extraordinarily slippery. It was hard to get a good footing on the rounded boulders, and the flat, smooth rocks were even worse. Jessie had been on frozen lakes that offered more traction. But it was only thirty yards; they would manage.

What made it all worse was the pointlessness of the effort. When they reached the base, then what? There was no possible way they could climb the solid granite wall. Even if they left the horses at the bottom, there weren't enough hand- or footholds to make it up the face of the cliff.

Midway through the boulder field Jessie decided she'd better mention her hesitance to Two Gun. "I hope you're not expecting me to climb that," she yelled ahead of her.

"You'll see," he answered knowingly.

When she got to the base of the wall she looked straight up. Standing underneath, it looked even more impressive and impossible to climb. The Kid read her thoughts.

"Uh-uh," he said with a smile. "Close your eyes, and count to ten."

"Then what?"

"You'll see."

Jessie didn't understand, but she closed her eyes and counted just the same. When she opened them, nothing was any clearer, except Two Gun and his horse were nowhere to be seen. "I don't see the point of hiding behind a boulder."

"Better 'n that," came the outlaw's voice. It sounded far away and had a hollow echo to it. "Close your eyes again."

"I'm in no mood to play hide-and-seek. I'm tired and cold . . ." she began, but she closed her eyes nonetheless.

"Howdy." His voice was loud in her ear. "Follow me," he said before she could ask any more questions.

He took Jessie's horse by the bridle and walked back behind a huge boulder. From where Jessie stood it seemed the rock lay flush to the granite wall. But there was about three feet of space between the two; just enough for a horse to squeeze through.

That was only the beginning of the surprise. The boulder hid from view a long vertical crack in the granite —a crack that was large enough to fit a man and a horse. Two Gun disappeared into it. Jessie followed him.

It was a dark passageway, but not pitch-black. Light was coming in from somewhere. Once her eyes grew accustomed to the gloom she could see a tunnel turn to the left. Around the end she expected the tunnel to open up into a larger cavern. An outlet in the cavern ceiling was probably the source of the light.

But when she turned the corner she was surprised. There was no cave, no underground vault safely hidden in the rock.

There was the sweet smell of damp woods. There was the sky, gray and raining. And all around there were high granite walls.

Jessie stepped out of the tunnel into a small box canyon. From the other side, the mountain had seemed solid, but looking around, Jessie could see the canyon was a narrow chasm between two huge granite slabs. Tucked in between the walls were trees, grass, and a small log cabin.

"It's simple, but I call it home. At least some of the time," Two Gun announced proudly as they walked up to the cabin.

Jessie was still impressed by the seclusion of the canyon. "I can see why you were anxious to get here."

"It's one of the few places I can feel really relaxed," he agreed as he pushed open the door. There was no lock on the door; obviously there was no call for one.

The cabin, in reality a one-room shack, had few furnishings and fewer amenities. Still, Jessie could tell someone had been there. The place was turned upside down. The woodpile had been scattered across the room, the straw mattress had been sliced through, and a board from the plank flooring had been ripped up. Someone had been here looking for something. That fact certainly did not avoid the outlaw. His face turned an ashen gray.

"Two Gun, are you all right?" Jessie asked with concern.

The outlaw was slow to answer. Jessie could understand. Two Gun's hideaway, his secret lair, was a secret no more. The one place he could go to be at ease had been violated.

"I want to show you something," he said finally. He grabbed a shovel that was behind the door, and they walked outside into the rain.

As they walked behind the shack, Jessie and Two Gun noticed the large holes that had been dug all over. Without any discernible pattern there were holes next to trees, boulders, and at the corners of the cabin.

"Someone's been busy," Jessie remarked dryly.

The Kid bent down to inspect one of the holes. It was filled with water, and the sides were caving in. "It's all mud. Impossible to tell how long ago they were dug. But they didn't get what they were looking for."

Jessie was going to ask what that was, but she had a pretty good idea. Anyway, she reckoned she would find out soon enough.

The Kid walked over to a large boulder. There were holes all around it. "But he came right close." He jumped down into the largest of the holes and began digging at the side wall, the one supporting the rock.

"Your shoulder," Jessie admonished. "Let me help."

"I'm all right. Besides, most of the work's done." He got down on his knees and started to dig at the soft mud

145

with his hands. A moment later he sat back and smiled. "I'll take that hand you were offerin'. . . ."

Jessie squatted down next to him. She could see a dark piece of leather sticking out through the mud. Two Gun scraped away more of the earth, and the little patch turned into what looked like the corner of a saddlebag.

"I think there's enough to grab hold of."

Jessie nodded, and together they tugged at the bag. It moved slightly, but still held fast. Two Gun scraped away more of the earth. "Let's try it again."

This time they were successful. But as the bag slipped out, Jessie lost her grip and went tumbling backward into the mud. A moment later Two Gun toppled back, and as he hit the ground, mud went splattering all across Jessie's face.

Two Gun leaned over and quickly began to wipe her face clean. "I'm sorry, Jessie," he began apologetically.

"It's only dirt. . . ."

"But it's on your face, and your skin is all . . . your skin is so smooth." His hand now was not so much wiping the mud from her face as caressing her soft cheek.

Jessie stared into his deep-brown eyes. His touch was warm and gentle.

Suddenly Two Gun scooped her up in his arms and pressed his lips to hers. The desire in the man's arms, his lips, his tongue, made Jessie tremble. She wrapped her arms around his neck, and ran her fingers through his curly dark hair.

That seemed to be all the encouragement Two Gun needed. With his lips still pressed against hers, his hands began to roam all over her body. Over her swelling bosom, down her sides, across her rounded buttocks, and across her thighs.

Jessie began to anticipate his touch. Her breasts would press against the palms of his hands. Her hips swayed and her legs spread. It was delightful and exasperating. His hands were everywhere and nowhere. She wanted his

146

hands to knead her breasts, to caress her thighs, to stroke her back. She wanted it all. And she wanted to feel it against her naked skin.

Her hands left his hair and moved to her shirt. The buttons were undone quickly, exposing her taut red nipples to Two Gun's fingers.

Jessie let out a gasp as his fingers found and pinched her hard buds. Then she threw back her head and sighed as his lips replaced his fingers. His tongue darted around and around the nipple as his hands kneaded the pale flesh of her breast.

The rain continued to fall, but neither of them paid it any attention. For Jessie's part, the moisture that was spreading between her legs was of more consequence than the rain that beat down against her bare skin. She was aware, violently aware, of the need to feel Two Gun press against her, to feel his weight on her, to feel his manhood in her. She could wait no longer.

Gently she pushed him away from her breasts and stood up. Two Gun looked at her and, misreading her actions, began to apologize profusely. "I don't know what came over me, Jessie. Well, I do, but I'm awfully sorry. I didn't mean to upset you none."

Jessie told him to shush, but there was no need to. As she began to wriggle out of her well-fitting jeans, Two Gun fell silent. His jaw dropped as her long, shapely legs stepped out of her pants. The tip of his tongue actually lolled out of the corner of his mouth at the sight of her thatch of curly blond hair. His eyes were riveted to her womanly mound.

His moment of inaction allowed Jessie to drop to her knees in front of the man and take hold of his belt buckle. Her fingers quickly undid the belt and top button, and then with a tug pulled down his pants. His throbbing member sprang free.

"It's even bigger than the night I first saw it," she said with admiration. She took his shaft in her hands, but after

147

one stroke changed her mind and lowered her face to it. Her hands went behind him and her fingers traced delicate patterns across his ass, as her tongue licked its way up his long barrel. Two Gun let out a loud groan. He sounded so appreciative that when Jessie reached the tip of his organ, she lowered her tongue and again ran it up his shaft.

He moaned again with such pleasure that Jessie stood up and pressed her body tightly to his. "I want you. Now," she purred huskily before planting her mouth to his.

She wasn't sure if she wrapped her legs around his and climbed up his torso, or if he grabbed her from behind and lifted her up. The only thing she was aware of was Two Gun's massive weapon pressing against the dew-soaked folds of her feminine flower. With a powerful thrust—was she pressing down or was he pushing up?—he entered her.

Nothing could describe the shock that shot through her body. The pleasure of it filled her totally, to the deepest recesses of her body. And it filled her again and again. Each stroke sent a new sensation, as pleasurable as the first, almost as satisfying as the next.

Jessie bounced joyously up and down on his shaft. She pressed her head into his neck, her mouth sucking against his muscular shoulder.

She was being swept away on an ocean of ecstasy. She was losing her balance, her sense of place. Her being centered around each stroke of Two Gun's firm pole. Then suddenly the world tilted.

Caught around the ankles by his own pants, the Kid lost his balance. Locked together, they fell heavily into the mud, and Two Gun continued to ride her with an even greater passion.

Jessie felt the ground oozing underneath her. But it was far from unpleasant. The mud offered a sensual resistance unequaled by even the finest feather mattress. It clung to her, held her, and caressed her like a thousand pairs of tiny hands.

Two Gun continued to ride her, faster and faster. Her

Chapter 14

Ki arrived at the Dixon place shortly after sunset. He knocked at the door, and after a moment Katie came to greet him. She took a quick look behind him; Ki smiled. "I'm alone," was all he had time for before Katie threw herself into his arms and gave him a long, lingering kiss.

She hurried him into the kitchen and gave him another kiss.

"Where's Nell?" Ki asked.

"Don't worry about Mama," she said with a confident smile. "She took to her bed right after supper."

"Is she all right?" he asked with concern.

"It's this weather. Affects her head something bad. And you're sopping wet." She seemed just now to have noticed it. "Wait right here and I'll fetch some of Daddy's clothes."

She was gone before Ki could utter another word. She returned a minute later, and immediately fell to the task of separating Ki from his wet things. As she pulled open his shirt she planted small kisses on his muscular chest. Slowly she worked her way down to his pants, where Ki's member

151

was already hard and throbbing.

On her knees, she started to stroke him through his pants. "Wait a minute, Katie. . . ."

"Don't worry, Mama's fast asleep," she repeated.

"That's not it. I came here for a reason," Ki said, perhaps a little too sharply.

Katie looked hurt. "You're saying you didn't come here for me?" But she wasn't all that offended; she released Ki's erect member from its confines and lowered her lips to his swollen tip.

"I couldn't lie," he said with a smile. "But you and your mother may be in danger here. There are men who might come to do you harm." He dropped to his knees and, as he kneeled on the floor opposite her, told her what he knew. "I think you and your mother should stay in town for a few days," he concluded.

"I think you're right," she agreed. "But I don't want to wake my mother and have her travelin' on a night like this. As long as you're here with us, we'll be safe."

Ki nodded.

"Good! Then you'll spend the night."

As his answer, Ki leaned over and kissed her hard. Katie met his fervor with a heat of her own, but after a moment broke away and rose to her feet. "If you do all those things I'm hoping you'll do, I don't expect to be able to keep my fool mouth shut," she said with unabashed glee. She took hold of his hand and, with a sensual squeeze, urged him to his feet. "It's only a short run to the barn."

They dashed through the rain, and within seconds were tumbling into the soft hay. Katie was not disappointed, and as she had professed, she pressed her face into Ki's muscular chest, where she proceeded to yell her fool head off most of the night.

In the morning, Ki hitched up the wagon and rode into town with Katie and Nell. At the fork a few miles outside of Coleville, Ki saw a gang of riders take the junction east.

Ki thought he recognized the lead rider as Tucker. But there was too much distance between them to be certain. The curious part was that the lead rider seemed to give him a long, hard look as well.

Ki fought the temptation to follow them. He wanted to see the Dixon women safely to town, and he wanted to speak with Jessie and the Two Gun Kid. And besides, if necessary, those many riders would be easy to trail.

Ki escorted the women to the house of their friend, then took his horse and hitched it to a rail outside the hotel. When he saw Jessie and the Kid were both gone, he left at once for the saloon. He was slightly concerned and figured if there was anything to tell he would get the straightest answers from Cooper. He only hoped the man was in.

It turned out the bartender was not only out, but the Silver Lode Saloon was locked shut. It was still early, and there was no reason to be suspicious, yet Ki felt a growing sense of urgency.

He walked his horse to the stables and, as he handed his horse to Wes, he remembered that Jessie had commented on the liveryman's friendly disposition toward the Two Gun Kid.

"What's been going on in town, Wes?" he asked casually. Wes gave him a shrewd look. "I've been gone the past few days," Ki explained.

Wes shook his head and told Ki of the incident involving the Kid and the sheriff.

"I saw some men riding out of town earlier."

"The posse."

"Tucker with them?"

"He's leading the crew." Wes spat into the dirt. "He's been appointed temporary sheriff."

Ki played a hunch. "A man named Collins with them?"

"Don't know any Collins." Wes thought a moment. "But I seem to recall Tucker calling someone by that name."

"And Jessie?" Ki asked expectantly.

Wes gave him a shrewd look. It was obvious to Ki the man knew something, but was debating whether to tell.

"She might be in trouble," Ki urged. "The Kid may be in trouble, too."

"You're a friend of Jessie's, ain't you?"

It was an unnecessary question; Wes knew that. But the man was leading up to something. Ki nodded. "A close friend."

"An' any friend of Jessie's is a friend of yours too, right?"

Again Ki nodded. He decided to lay his cards on the table. "Wes, I don't believe the Kid is a killer. I don't think he gunned down the sheriff in cold blood, and I don't think he killed the marshal either. But I think he and Jessie may need help."

Wes nodded. "She took off after the Kid yesterday."

"Do you know where they were heading?"

Wes nodded. "But they won't be there today. You won't find 'em, and the posse won't either." Nevertheless, Wes told Ki about the old mill.

"One more question, Wes. Know anything about the Coleville General Store?"

"Ain't much to know. Hollowell owns it, and one way or another it'll soon be the only general store in town."

"Why is that?"

"Easy credit," Wes answered flatly.

Ki thought that over. "There's no such thing as easy credit."

"Folks'll soon find that out, but once they do, it'll be too late. I know Hollowell's game. Once he puts Olsen's store out of business, he'll jack up the prices, and folks'll have no choice but to pay him."

Ki agreed, but he was thinking about that safe he had seen tucked away under the counter of the general store. "Wes, could you saddle me a fresh horse and hitch it up outside the store?"

"The Coleville General Store?" Wes said with a twinkle in his eye.

Ki nodded. "The sooner the better."

"Five minutes an' the fastest Appaloosa you ever laid eyes on'll be there waiting."

With a nod of appreciation, Ki turned and left the stable. He had planned to take a look at the store's safe, but midnight had seemed a better time to come calling. Unfortunately, Ki no longer had the luxury of waiting till then. He wanted to get right on Tucker's trail.

Ki entered the general store. Luckily, it was empty, save for the clerk who was behind the counter. Ki sized up the man quickly. He looked to be in his mid-forties, and had the lean look of an ex-cowpuncher as opposed to the softer look of a lifelong merchant. Ki guessed the man could take care of himself; Ki only hoped he wouldn't try anything foolish.

"You were closed the other night, but I helped myself to two cans of beans and a can of tomatoes. I'd like to pay for them now," Ki said as he stepped up to the counter.

The clerk showed surprise. "I can't say as how I condone breakin' into a store, but I respect yer honesty, fella."

"I also hope you respect this," Ki said as he pulled Tucker's revolver from his waistband. "Open the safe."

"If'n yer lookin' for money you'd be better off holdin' up the bank," the clerk snapped. "There's no money in there."

"Then you shouldn't mind having me take a look. Open it! Now!" Ki edged around to the side of the counter, where he could keep a steely eye on the man's every move.

The clerk bent down and opened the safe. When Ki realized what might happen it was too late to prevent it.

The door of the safe opened out toward Ki. For an instant the clerk's hands were hidden by the door. It was one of the oldest tricks, hiding a gun in a safe, though again it amazed Ki that someone would try to outgun a man who

155

already had the drop on him. All Ki had to do was squeeze the trigger. It only took one finger to blow away the clerk, yet the man gambled that he could pull out his arm, raise the gun, and aim it true, before Ki's finger would jerk barely half an inch. The gamble didn't pay off.

The split-second advance warning Ki had was the only thing that saved the clerk's life. It gave Ki the opportunity to shift the gun ever so slightly. Instead of blowing away the clerk's face, he put a hole into the man's shoulder. The clerk toppled backward, clutching his shoulder and cursing. It was a messy wound, but the man would live. Ki picked up the clerk's sixgun, stuck it into his waistband, then peered into the safe. A packet of papers was the only contents. Ki placed the clothbound packet into his shirt pocket and calmly walked to the door.

As promised, the Appaloosa was tethered and waiting. Ki swung into the saddle and casually walked the horse into the rear alley. But once out of sight they quickly kicked up some dust.

A few miles from town, Ki slowed his horse. The same thing that had made him hurry also allowed him to stop. Initially, Ki had wanted to get out of town quickly, before complications from shooting the clerk could arise. But then he had realized that anyone capable of coming after him was probably already out chasing the Two Gun Kid. So Ki had the liberty of stopping, and although he also had a strong desire to overtake the posse as soon as possible, he reasoned that a momentary look at the papers in his pocket would not slow him down terribly.

At first glance, the papers appeared to be standard IOUs. Though the notes seemed rather fancy in their meticulous type, there was nothing particularly suspicious about any of them, till he got to the last one. Then Ki realized what was wrong.

Each of the notes had a significant space above the borrower's signature. Ki had noticed it but thought nothing of it. Nor, no doubt, had any of the people who had signed them. But the last note, signed by Eugene Dixon, had one significant difference. There was no space between the body of the note and the signature. The space was occupied by one more paragraph. The extra clause agreed that the noteholder—one Randolph Hollowell—when calling in the IOU had the option, upon default, of purchasing the stated collateral for a fixed price. Though Ki got the gist of it immediately, he read the note again from top to bottom.

In essence, Eugene Dixon agreed that if he couldn't pay the note when it was due, he would sell Hollowell his land at an agreed price. Ki didn't have to know the size of Dixon's spread or the going rate in these parts to know the price was grossly undervalued. Though all legal, Hollowell would be getting the ranch at a steal.

Ki didn't have to know the marshal personally to know that he never would have agreed to those terms. The other notes were all the proof he needed. Though Eugene Dixon had signed the paper Ki held in his hand, he had never signed away the rights to his land. It was a simple but clever scam; had Ki only seen one IOU he never would have caught on. First, Hollowell obtained the signatures on the straightforward notes, then he reprinted them with the addition of that last clause, the poisoned paragraph. All one needed was an outward front full of goodwill, and a hand printing press. The competition between the two general stores and the access to easy credit at Hollowell's store provided the first. And Ki had no doubt the back room of the Hollowell-owned printing shop provided the second.

He stuffed the papers back into his shirt and once again gave the Appaloosa its head.

Ki approached the old mill with caution. But Wes was right. The Two Gun Kid was not there and neither was the posse.

Though Ki had no difficulty trailing Tucker and his cohorts, the same could not be said about their luck tracking the Two Gun Kid. The posse was obviously having a hard time. Their tracks would head off one way, then a bit later double back and start out in another direction. After a while Ki discerned a pattern. The posse seemed to be moving steadily north, but would periodically verge off. It was as if they suspected the general direction the Kid would be moving in, but checked nevertheless for signs that he might have changed course.

After a while Ki took a chance and ignored the tracks of the posse. He struck out due north on a course he hoped would bring him closer to the Kid, or help him overtake the posse.

Ki was just beginning to think he had made a tactical error when he heard shots behind him and to the right. Ki reeled his horse around and bolted off in that direction.

It turned out he had overshot the posse. Either Ki had made better time than he had realized, or the posse had stopped to eat and to rest their horses.

The gunfire, continuing at a hectic rate, guided Ki directly to the grassy ravine that was the scene of the shootout.

From the looks of things the posse had stopped to rest when they were attacked from the top of the wooded hill. It was a good place to lay an ambush, but it seemed the attackers were greatly outnumbered. In fact, there seemed to be only a single gunman. But by moving from tree to tree and firing quickly but accurately, he was able to keep the posse at bay.

Ki couldn't get a good look at who the man was. But he immediately discounted the Two Gun Kid. Even though the outlaw was admittedly fond of having the hunters become the hunted, Ki reasoned the outlaw's injured shoulder would not let him move and shoot that well. He also suspected that if it were the Kid, Jessie would be up there with him. Ki smiled to himself. He would have liked to see the Kid explain to Jessie that she should stay behind because a gunfight was no place for a lady.

Ki had his suspicions as to the identity of the man, but any man who opposed Tucker and his posse was a friend of the outlaw's and, as Ki saw it, a friend of his as well.

He took out his gun and crawled up through the woods. Though it would be deadly to catch the posse in a cross fire, Ki held back. He wanted to know a little more about the situation before he tipped his hand. A few minutes later he was glad he had waited.

There were eight horses tethered together. Even checking twice, Ki counted only six men. The conclusion was obvious. Two men were circling around to come up behind their attacker. Ki moved back quickly, and started to circle to his right. Maybe he could overtake the two men from the posse. No one was shooting at him, so he could afford to be a little less cautious, whereas the two plug-uglies would be moving very carefully and slowly indeed.

But his hopes vanished when he heard someone cry out, "Hold yer fire, Collins. We got him."

The attacker emerged from behind an evergreen, the plug-uglies' guns pointing directly at his back.

It was fortunate that Ki had listened to that inner voice and had resisted the impulse to go in shooting. Even if he had kept the body of the posse pinned down, the two plug-uglies still would have gotten the drop on the attacker. But now, with his presence unknown, there was a chance Ki could free the man who had tried to stop the posse single-handedly. It would be only fitting, after what the bartender had done for him, that Ki should return the favor and save Cooper from the hands of the posse.

They pushed Cooper into the clearing. A big man with a pockmarked face that was twisted into a perpetual snarl strode up to Cooper. Ki guessed him to be Collins.

Collins stopped face-to-face with Cooper, then his right palm shot out, smacking loudly into Cooper's face. The bartender's head jerked with the impact of the slap. "Where's the Kid?" the rustler demanded.

159

There was no answer, and Collins's left hand came across with another powerful slap. "Where is he?" he repeated angrily.

"Go easy with him, Collins," one of the plug-uglies warned. "Tucker wants him alive, remember."

Collins didn't even turn to the man; he kept his stare on Cooper. "He'll take an awful beating, but he'll be alive. Now, where is the Kid?"

"I wouldn't tell you if I knew," Cooper said contemptuously.

He barely got the words out before Collins's fist slammed into his gut. He doubled over.

Ki had seen enough. He pulled out the clerk's revolver from his waistband.

"Maybe he doesn't know where the Kid is," one of the posse remarked to Collins.

"They're not all as stupid as you, Collins," Cooper began, but was silenced by another crushing blow to his gut. "If I knew where the Kid was, why would I be here now?" he said between painful breaths.

"Maybe he's got a point," agreed one of the posse.

Cooper gave him a thoughtful look, then seemed to make up his mind. "I don't know where the Kid is, but Tucker does."

"Tucker!"

Cooper nodded. "Why else would he go on ahead, and leave you all to fight me?"

"Don't make sense," remarked another of the posse.

"Sure it does," Cooper said as he turned to him.

"Why?" This time it was Collins who asked.

"For the money. Tucker wants the loot for himself. Why share it with you all?"

"That skunk." Collins studied Cooper carefully. "Then why would he care about taking you alive?"

"Because he's not sure where the money is."

A slow, ugly smile spread across Collins's face. "I'm givin' you two seconds to tell us where the money's at."

"If I knew, would I be here?" Cooper said with a phony chuckle.

It made perfect sense even to Collins. The plug-ugly's hand slid down to his holster. "Well, if'n you don't know where the Kid is, and you don't know where the money's at, I see no reason to keep you alive." His hand slipped his sixgun out.

It never cleared its holster.

A shot rang out from the trees, and Collins dropped to the dirt.

Ki stepped out, brandishing a revolver in each hand. "No one move." He kept a watchful eye on all the men, but addressed Cooper. "Get their guns."

He looked down at Collins. The man was hurt bad, but was still alive. Ki placed one of his guns back into his waistband. He felt better having his hands, weapons in their own right, unencumbered. He disliked guns, perhaps because he felt he didn't have total and exact control over them. For a brief moment he wished he had considered improving his shooting skill. If he could shoot a gun from a man's hand, he could have avoided serious injury to the store clerk and Collins. He recalled the time his friend Stoney had shot off the trigger finger of that plug-ugly up in Oregon. . . .

Ki admonished himself immediately. This was no time to go strolling down memory lane. He turned to Cooper, who had just collected all their guns. "Keep an eye on them. I'll get some rope." He put the second gun in his waistband and walked over to the horses. But before he got even halfway there, he heard Collins call out to him.

"Hold it, Chinaman! Drop those guns."

Ki turned around slowly. Collins had been lying face-down in the dirt. Cooper never even thought to keep an eye on him; he never heard the rustler struggle to his feet. But now Collins, on shaky feet, stood behind the bartender. And there was nothing shaky about his pistol. The barrel of his gun dug smartly into the bartender's temple.

161

★

Chapter 15

They slept till the unheard-of hour of noon. There was no sun creeping in to wake them, but even so it was unlikely either Jessie or Two Gun would have stirred. They had been up almost the whole night. The Kid was a man of his word.

The smell of flapjacks in the pan urged Jessie awake. "Mmm, smells good," she said dreamily.

"Beans an' flatcakes. There wasn't much else in stock," he said with an apologetic smile.

"It'll be fine," Jessie said as she got dressed.

Two Gun brought over two plates of food. "Now, while I still got a mind to, there's some things that need discussin'."

"All right."

Two Gun reached over for the saddlebag that they had pulled out from the mud. Jessie could see the leather was stamped HOLLOWELL FREIGHT COMPANY. "First, I want you to take this." Jessie shook her head. "It's not blood money, Jessie," the outlaw explained. "I didn't take it from any

"I'll tell you as we saddle up."

"Where are we going?"

"Back to town. But not together."

"Two Gun, I can take care of myself. I told you I'm skilled at quite a few things." She pulled her Colt from its holster. "See that knot on that pine tree?"

"Don't, Jessie!" he snapped. "I believe you," he said in a gentle voice. "Especially after last night," he added with a smile. "But there might be a posse anywhere near here. A shot could bring 'em right to our door."

Jessie looked at the outlaw with much respect. The man was good; a professional at his trade. "Two Gun, I'm amazed the law ever caught up with you," she remarked offhandedly.

The Kid shrugged. "Nothin' much you can do when you're betrayed."

"Except get even?"

The Kid ignored the question. He went back to the cabin and started to saddle up their horses.

"It's true," he started at length. "I came here to find out who betrayed me, but you can never get even." He tightened the cinches as he talked, refusing to look at Jessie as he told his story. "I became an outlaw to get even. My father owned a small deed company. Hollowell swindled him, left him penniless, but even worse, disgraced him. My father was a broken man the day he packed his gun over to Hollowell's house. They called it self-defense, but it was suicide. My father wasn't too good with firearms. He was shot dead by one of Hollowell's men."

Jessie wanted to express her sympathy, but chose not to interrupt.

"I wanted to gun down that bastard more than anything. Trouble is, someone beat me to it. He was shot a few days later cheating at cards. But he was just a tool of Hollowell's, anyhow. I should have just killed Old Man Hollowell then."

"But that would have been murder," Jessie said softly.

165

He turned to her. "Maybe that bothered me some too, but I thought it would be better to bleed him first. Steal the thing he loved most, his money. So I started robbing his banks, his freight company . . . and the rest, the rest was just playing out the hand I dealt myself."

"And now you're going back to finish what you started," Jessie said angrily.

Two Gun shook his head slowly. "That won't bring back my father," he said sadly. "There's just no way you can get even on a score like that."

"Then why go back to town?"

"'Cause the hand's been dealt an' I ain't folding."

"Why go through with it, Two Gun? They'll hang you for murder."

"Justice." He could see she didn't understand. "I think Hollowell shot the marshal."

"The old man?" Jessie said incredulously.

"His son Luke."

"Why didn't you say this before?"

"I didn't know it before," he answered with just the slightest trace of mockery. "It wasn't till the sheriff came gunning for you that I began to suspect."

"I'm still not certain why that happened."

"It happened because you knew too much, because you might be stumbling onto the truth."

"Why would the sheriff—"

Two Gun didn't even wait for her to finish the question. "Hollowell owns just about everything of importance in town. Why shouldn't he also own the sheriff?"

"All right, but why would Hollowell shoot the marshal, or rather come gunning for you in the first place?"

"Maybe he thought I was coming after his pa, or maybe when he couldn't find his money he got so blasted angry he just couldn't wait to put some slugs into me."

"Just one other question. How did Hollowell know about your hideout?"

"Maybe he found it by accident, or maybe the person

166

the two grappled on the ground, Ki got his respiration back to normal. The two men continued to roll on the ground. The rustler was every bit as strong as Ki, if not a few pounds heavier.

After several pointless reversals of position, Ki feigned fatigue and allowed his opponent to roll on top of him. The man was quick to seize the advantage, delivering a strong blow to Ki's head. Ki rolled with the punch as best he could, but he still felt his ears ringing. As the man drew back his fist for another blow, Ki grabbed him by the shirt and brought his knee up hard into his opponent's ass. He went tumbling over headfirst. Ki scrambled up, then dropped down hard, knee into the man's solar plexus. Before his opponent could recover Ki's two arms spread out wide, and his hands, hard edge first, came crashing down into the man's neck. Ki aimed for that *atemi* point that lay just under the ears. But he needn't have worried about being precise. The force of the blow would make up for any minor error. The man's head jerked on impact, then sagged to one side as the force on the pressure point rendered him unconscious.

Now, if only Cooper was holding his own. Ki jumped up and raced to the aid of his friend.

As it turned out, Cooper was holding his ground. He had a keen eye and quick fists that managed to keep his three opponents at bay, though it was doubtful how long he could hold them off. His face was already bloody from the exchange of blows.

The three men were circling around Cooper waiting for an opening when Ki rushed up. He doubled his fists and, with a yell, hit the first man in the kidneys. A combination double *yoko-geri-keage* and *mae-geri-keage*—a perfectly executed side-kick delivered first to the ribs, then, without fully redrawing, to the face, followed by a forward snap-kick to the head—took care of the second man. The first, still doubled over, was staggering to his feet, when a spinning-wheel kick ended his fight.

171

Cooper was delivering powerful one-twos to the face and body of the final opponent. The man kept to his feet, but the fight was out of him. One last uppercut knocked him flat onto the grass. He didn't get up. The fight was over.

Cooper wiped the blood from his mouth. "Thanks, Ki."

"You would have done the same. . . ."

Cooper looked around at the bodies that dotted the grass. "I might have tried, but quite frankly, I don't think I could have."

"It just takes a little practice," Ki said with a touch of humor.

"Now I see why you don't lay much stock in simple guns," Cooper said as he looked down at the *shuriken* that had killed Collins. "But did you ever think you might have missed and killed me?" he mused aloud.

It had never entered Ki's mind, but he didn't say that. Instead Ki pointed to Collins. "When you tried to knock away his gun, you might have gotten me shot."

"I didn't have a choice, he was going to kill you. . . ."

"Exactly." Ki had made his point. Cooper acknowledged it with a comprehending smile.

They quickly tied up the remains of the posse, then mounted up.

"Do you know where the Kid is?" Ki asked.

Cooper shook his head. "Not exactly, but I have a rough idea."

"And Tucker?"

"He's got the same idea."

Tucker tied his horse to a tree, slipped a scattergun from its boot, and started across the boulder field on foot. All the Kid's planning, all his friends, and all his skill couldn't save him now. Tucker was heady with the taste of victory. He slipped on a rock and skinned his palm. He cursed out loud, then gave a wild laugh that held no humor. The cut on his hand didn't matter; it didn't bother him. Nothing would bother him again. Soon everyone would know who was the best gunman. After he killed the Kid he would get the respect he had long deserved. He was going to enjoy watching the Kid die. . . .

Two Gun turned in the saddle, and took one last look at his little canyon. The shack he had built himself, the trees he had sat under, the rock formations he'd spent many a lazy afternoon staring at. "There are a lot of memories connected to this place." His voice was thick. "But the one that'll stick, the one I'll remember most, happened last night, with you."

Jessie brought her horse up alongside his. "Two Gun," she began softly.

"Wait. Before I lose the gumption to, and before it's too late, there's something I've got to say. I've wanted to tell you since, well, maybe since we first kissed. But especially after last night. . . ."

"There's no need to say anything, Two Gun."

"Delbert Fenster."

"What?"

"I wasn't always the Two Gun Kid," he said defensively. "My name's Delbert Fenster."

Jessie looked at the Kid. His face was a curious mix of pride and embarrassment. Tears welled up in her eyes. She leaned over and hugged him tight. "Delbert, Delbert Fenster. . . ." She was laughing and crying at the same time.

"Go easy on it, Jessie. I haven't heard it in years."

"There was only one thing I really wanted to know about you. From that first night I nursed you, I wanted to know your real name."

"There aren't many who know me by that name. I can count 'em on one hand. I wanted you to be one of them."

Jessie stroked his hair and looked into his eyes. She wanted to say so much, but she couldn't find the words. Perhaps most of all she wanted to tell him to be careful.

"Don't say anything, Jessie." The Kid took her hand, kissed it, then gently pulled it away. "There are things that need doin'." And with that he entered the rock tunnel.

Coming out the other side, he sensed something was wrong, but too late.

"Hands up, Kid, or the lady gets a headful of buck-shot!"

speaking. "It's been a long time," was all he said, but the words held much feeling.

Jessie nodded. "I understand, Two Gun."

But she didn't. The Kid shook his head. "Not that," he said with a smile. "That was the very first thing I did after prison. It's been a long time since . . . since I've been with a woman I cared for."

The simple statement of affection had a profound effect on her. She wanted to explain that to him, to tell him she cared too, but more than anything it seemed she wanted to make love to him again.

"There are things I have to tell you, Jessie . . ."

"Not now, Two Gun." The passion was stirring within her loins. "Lie down next to me," she said softly.

The Kid understood. He bent down to kiss her neck, then slowly inched his lips down her body. Jessie parted her legs, and the Kid's tongue followed the contours of her body. Jessie closed her eyes and let out a soft moan.

After a while Two Gun raised his head from between her legs. "I said we'd have all the time in the world. I don't plan to let you make a liar out of me." Jessie could feel his hardened manhood lying heavy against her thigh.

"I wouldn't plan on doing such a thing," she said, as she licked her lips in anticipation.

hips moved with his, her fingers dug into him and pulled him even tighter, and he continued thrusting deeply into her. Her breaths came in short gasps. Her eyes closed tight, her face screwed up, not in pain, but in total, complete rapture.

Two Gun looked down into her face. "Oh, Jessie. You are so beautiful, so beautiful," he began to repeat over and over.

Jessie would have thought it impossible, but Two Gun seemed to swell even more. Her hips began to buck wildly. Her inner muscles, this time of their own accord, began to grip his shaft tighter and tighter. She squeezed every inch of him till he screamed out. It was a long, joyous wail.

And when she felt him begin to pump himself deep inside her she climaxed. With the first spasm Jessie gave out a little shriek. But Two Gun continued to pound her body. She felt his muscle pump again, and her body reacted. The second tremor, more devastating, took hold of her and wouldn't let go. She threw back her head and screamed into the rain. She continued her cry until Two Gun, an eternity later, lay silently on top of her.

That the rain continued to fall and the canyon walls remained standing as tall and straight as before surprised Jessie. Surely the world was coming apart at the seams. She had even felt the ground move under her. In blissful repose she contemplated the wonder. . . .

"Let's get you inside and in front of a warm fire," Two Gun said as he slid off her. He grabbed the leather saddlebag, then scooped Jessie up in his arms and carried her to the shack.

Though Jessie still felt the warmth emanating from deep within her body, the heat from the fire felt good on her naked skin. She leaned back and stretched out her shapely body in front of the stone hearth.

Two Gun came and sat down next to her. He took her head in his hands and studied her for a long moment before

149

common folk. It's all Hollowell's—an' there ain't an honest dollar in the whole bag."

Two Gun misunderstood part of her objection. "I don't want money for helping you, Two Gun. That's not why I did it."

"I know that, Jessie. I misjudged you once, but—"

"And besides, I don't need it."

"I hope you don't take this wrong," he began uneasily, "but I wasn't giving it all to you."

"Oh."

"I want you to take it and split it four ways. Wes, Cooper, yourself . . . and the Widow Dixon."

Jessie was moved by the gesture. "That's very considerate—" she started to say, but stopped as Two Gun continued talking.

"Wes is an old man; he deserves better than workin' at the stables. And I'd like to see Cooper buy back the other half of the Silver Lode. They've both helped me out of tight jams. They deserve something."

"I'm sure they didn't do it for the money either, Two Gun."

"I know that, Jessie. They're good men."

"We help because we're your friends."

The outlaw smiled "That's why I want them to have the money. And if it weren't for me, Nell Dixon would still have her man. Someone had better help out with the bills."

Jessie didn't like his tone. He was sounding like a condemned man making out his last will and testament. "Two Gun, you're not planning on doing anything foolish?"

"I just want to explain some things."

That didn't exactly answer her question. "Then explain how you got the money under that boulder," she said lightheartedly, hoping to change the pervading air of gloom.

"Easy. When you finish I'll take you round back and show you."

Jessie shoved the last bite of flapjacks into her mouth.

She was suddenly eager to get out of the oppressive shack. "Finished," she announced with her mouth full, and went to the door.

"Leverage," Two Gun said as he pointed to the boulder. "See that small rock there?" Jessie nodded; there was a smaller rock about six feet from the boulder. "Well, there's a small tree trunk somewhere back there that I used to pry up the boulder. There's a fancy word for it I heard once . . ."

"Fulcrum."

"Yeah, that's it," he said with a smile. "Worked like a charm. Didn't take much effort at all."

Jessie could understand; she could even picture it. "That's how you lifted the boulder, but how did you slip the bag under it?"

"I sat on the log, then tossed the bag under."

"Then who else knew there was money there?" Inadvertently, she realized, she had asked the wrong question. The Kid had slipped back into his somber mood.

"I'll soon find out."

Jessie noticed that he used the singular pronoun. "I'm in this, too," she protested.

The Kid shook his head. "If anything happens to me I want to make sure that money gets back to the people who deserve it."

"I see what you're saying, Two Gun, but I'm not going to desert you."

"Jessie!" the outlaw snapped. "This is important. Those people, especially Nell Dixon, really need that money."

"Then you give it to them."

"I have things to do," the outlaw answered flatly.

"Like . . . ?" Jessie challenged. "You know more than you've told," she accused.

"I reckon so," he said with a heavy sigh. "But I wasn't holding nothin' back. The pieces just started to fit."

Jessie looked at him expectantly. "Well?"

who betrayed me told him. Someone had to be handing out money, or no one would have squealed," he added in answer to her next question.

"And how would that person know about the hideaway?"

"There are ways to find out just about anything," he said simply. "Nothing can remain a perfect secret for long." He swung up into his saddle.

Jessie took hold of his bridle. "Then let the law, not some appointed sheriff, but the real law, a district marshal, take care of Hollowell."

"There's only one real law I know of."

He didn't have to pat his guns; Jessie got his meaning. Jessie mounted her horse. "Then I'm coming with you."

"Don't!"

"I thought you believed me when I said I can take care of myself."

"I did, and that's why I trust you to make it back to town without me." He set his horse in motion.

"I can be as stubborn as you, Mr. Two Gun Kid," Jessie snapped as she had her horse fall into step behind his.

"All right, but at the first sign of trouble I want you burning the breeze."

Jessie promised nothing. She would cross that bridge when she came to it.

Ki let out the most cold-blooded laugh he could muster. With his back still turned to Collins he slipped a *shuriken* into his palm. "I'm no fool, Collins. I figure it's him or me."

"I'll kill him sure as I'm breathing," Collins warned again. "Throw down your guns and you can both walk away."

Ki didn't believe him for a moment, and though he hated to gamble with Cooper's life, it was the only way. He turned around slowly. "If you think you can blow out his brains and get me, too, you're welcome to try." Ki would never sacrifice the life of another to save his own, but he had to make Collins believe he would.

Collins let out a laugh as he slipped his forearm around Cooper's neck and pulled the bartender close. Cooper's body shielded everything but Collins's head. Collins was making it plain he was ready to go all the way with this. "All right, Chinaman. I'm willin' to test yer aim."

"You're brave, I'll give you that, but you're damn stupid, too."

Collins reddened at the insult. "I'll remember that when we're buryin' you."

"Cooper's a dead man," Ki pronounced flatly. "If you think a dead man will save your life, you're a bigger fool than Larsen." The mention of the other rustler brought a gasp from one of the posse. Ki was pleased with himself for throwing out that tidbit. It helped to increase the tension in the air. And the tension was working for Ki.

Only the tension kept Collins and the rest of the posse immobilized. If any of the others were to rush him simultaneously, or make a dash for their guns that were lying only a few yards away, Ki would be helpless. He could get one or two, but that would be the end. But it simply came down to the fact that no one wanted to gamble on being *the* one—Collins included. In the split second that he gave it thought, he realized there might be another reason Collins didn't just shoot him when he had the chance to. Greed had gotten to the man. Collins was afraid of shooting someone who might know something about the Kid's whereabouts, or more specifically the whereabouts of the outlaw's hidden stash.

Collins looked directly at Ki. "What's Larsen got to do with this?"

"Didn't Buck tell you?" Ki said amiably "Larsen thought he could outdraw me, too." The news had a sobering effect on Collins. Ki could see him tighten his grip around Cooper's neck. "Like I was saying," Ki continued calmly, "Cooper's a dead man. I can put all six bullets into his neck. At this range four will go through and slam into your chest, Collins. It only takes one to find your heart." Poker was not the only game you could bluff in.

"I ain't got no fight with you, Chinaman. Throw down your gun, and you'll live to see the sun set."

Ki felt he had pushed just about as far as he could. "How do I know I can believe you, Collins?"

"I got no reason to lie. And I'll give you my word." Collins gave such a forced smile that even if Ki were inclined to believe the man, the smile would have changed his mind instantly.

"Don't believe him, Ki," Cooper yelled out. The grip around his neck tightened. "He's a liar . . ." he gasped before losing his voice.

"Don't pay him no mind, Ki," Collins said. Again there was that reassuring smile that was anything but.

"I'm taking you for a man of your word, Collins." Ki's hand went to his guns. Midway there Collins stopped him.

"Left hand, Chinaman."

The suited Ki just fine. His right hand remained poised in front of him as his left hand went to his gun, pulled it out, and dropped it in the dirt.

"Now the other one," Collins ordered.

"I won't feel quite the same without my guns. You know how a man gets used to carrying those things with him."

Ki had not made the comment to gain sympathy from the rustler; he said it to tip off Cooper. It was the verbal equivalent of a wink. He was positive the bartender would remember the first night Ki came into the saloon—without any guns. He just hoped Cooper would know what to do.

"You'll live," Collins said with a nasty chuckle.

"I expect so," Ki said honestly, though he knew Collins was planning otherwise. The next second would prove Ki right or wrong.

Ki pulled out the gun and flamboyantly tossed it aside. At the movement, Ki saw Collins's eyes follow his hand.

In that instant, Ki flicked his right wrist and sent the *shuriken* on its deadly mission.

As soon as Ki tossed the gun aside, Collins transferred the gun from Cooper's temple and pointed it at Ki. His lips pulled back in a thin smile; it was a smile that lasted the rest of his life.

The minute Cooper felt the pressure ease from his head, his right elbow shot up into his captor's arm. He knew what Collins intended to do. He had to save Ki somehow.

The shot went off into the air, and Collins mysteriously toppled backward. He was dead even before his gun went off. The shiny silver throwing star dug deep into the man's brain, one edge barely protruding from a bloody eye socket.

And then the fighting began.

As if released from a trance, the men of the posse rushed to their guns. Cooper had the presence of mind to bend down and pick up Collins's gun. He fired into the crowd. That stopped them briefly. Two men dropped, then the hammer fell on an empty chamber, and a free-for-all broke out.

Though Ki and Cooper were outnumbered five to two, it was anything but a fair fight. Three men rushed Cooper, and two came at Ki.

The first of Ki's assailants found his jaw broken as a high-flying kick exploded in his face. Ki landed quickly and a snapping side-kick knocked down his second opponent. Ki turned around. The first man was nursing his jaw, but moving closer. Ki had no time to waste. He wanted to dispose of his attackers as fast as possible, and get over to help Cooper. Ki struck out with a volley of lightning punches. Two straight jabs to the chin sent the man into excruciating pain. Then a final roundhouse knocked him to the ground, unconscious.

Ki turned again to face his other adversary, when he was thrown backward by the charging man. Striking with the force of a bull, the man knocked the breath from Ki. But as

170